TIGER MOTH

The Fortune Cookies of Weevil

Librarian Reviewer
Allyson A. W. Lyga, MS
Library Media/Graphic Novel Consultant
Fulbright Memorial Fund Scholar, author

Reading Consultant
Elizabeth Stedem
Educator/Consultant, Colorado Springs, CO
MA in Elementary Education, University of Denver, CO

STONE ARCH BOOKS
MINNEAPOLIS   SAN DIEGO

Graphic Sparks are published by Stone Arch Books,
151 Good Counsel Drive, P.O. Box 669,
Mankato, Minnesota 56002.
www.stonearchbooks.com

Library of Congress Cataloging-in-Publication Data
Reynolds, Aaron, 1970–
    The Fortune Cookies of Weevil / by Aaron Reynolds; illustrated by Erik Lervold.
    p. cm. — (Graphic Sparks. Tiger Moth)
    ISBN-13: 978-1-59889-318-2 (library binding)
    ISBN-10: 1-59889-318-1 (library binding)
    ISBN-13: 978-1-59889-413-4 (paperback)
    ISBN-10: 1-59889-413-7 (paperback)
    1. Graphic novels. I. Lervold, Erik. II. Title.
PN6727.R45F67 2007
741.5'973—dc22   2006028029

Summary: Who is sending all those fortune cookies around the city? What sinister message
is tucked inside? Why are the dreaded Scorpions working with the Yellow Jacket Hive?
Fourth-grade ninjas, Tiger Moth and his best buddy King Pow, smell something crummy
in the air, and it's not the jumbo hot chocolate from Starbugs!

Art Director: Heather Kindseth
Graphic Designer: Brann Garvey

1 2 3 4 5 6 12 11 10 09 08 07

Printed in the United States of America

TIGER MOTH

The Fortune Cookies of Weevil

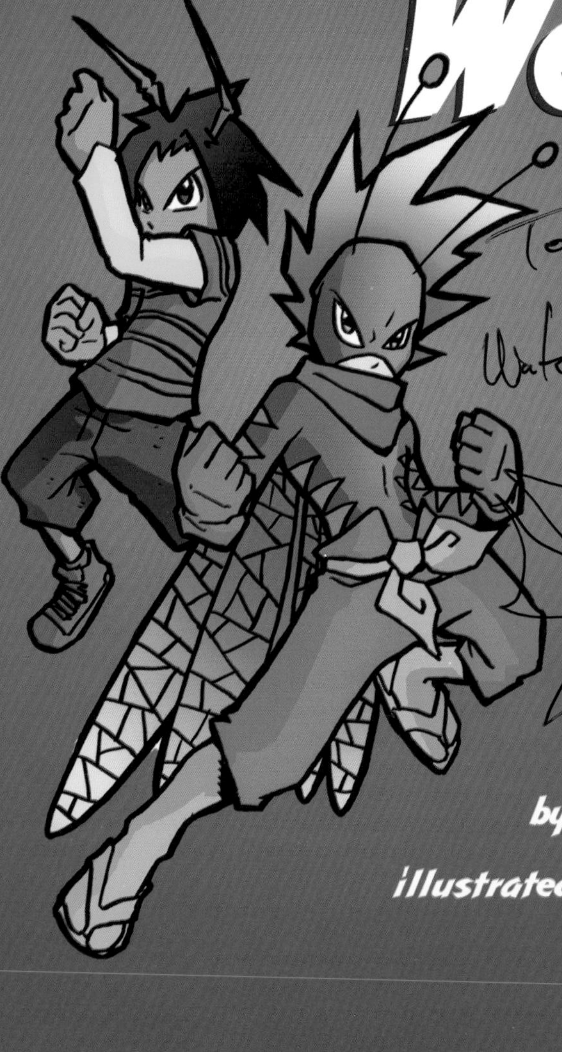

To Kevin,
Watch out for the spicy Kung Pow!
01-28-09

by Aaron Reynolds

illustrated by Erik Lervold

Cast of Characters

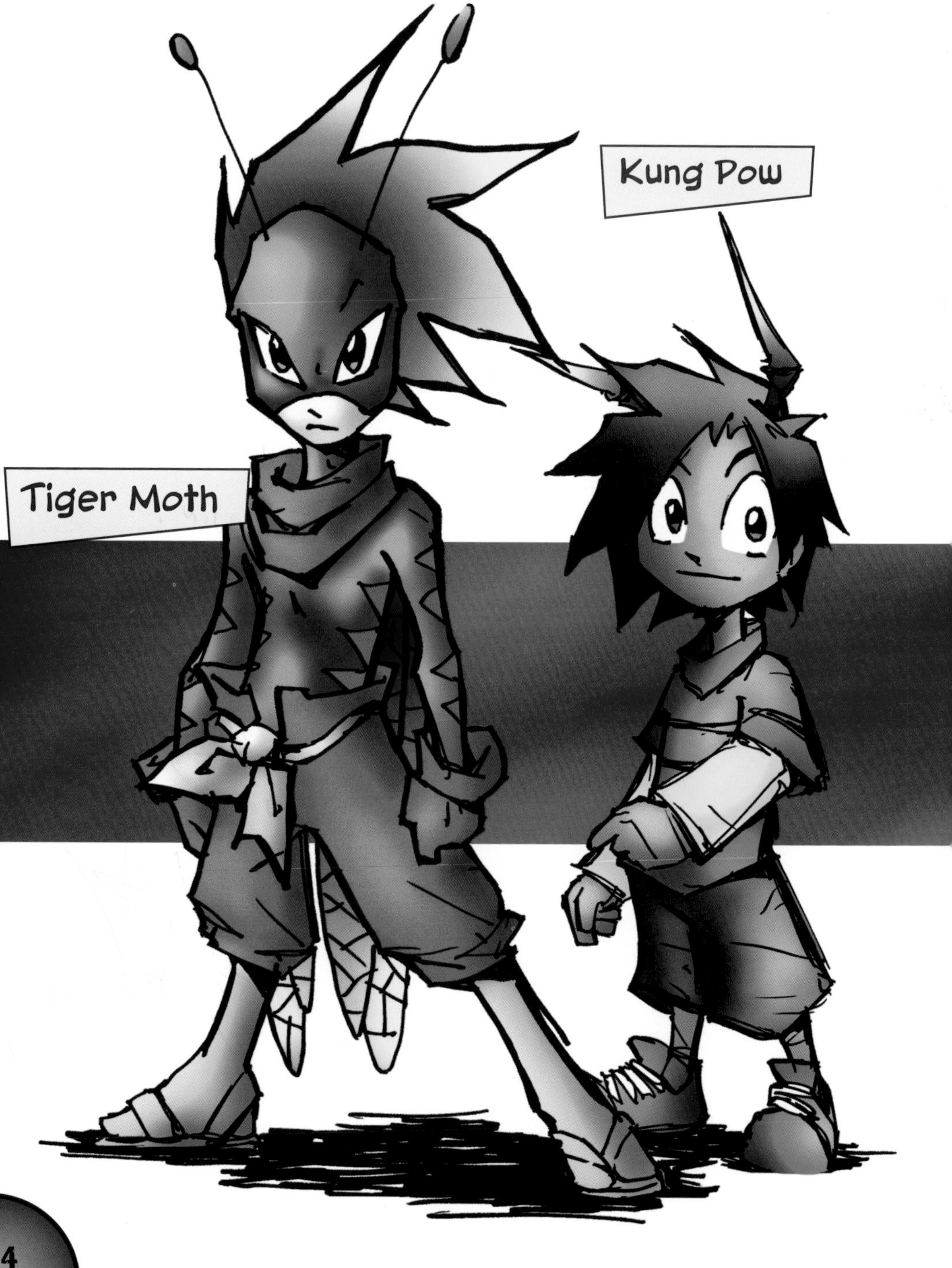
Kung Pow
Tiger Moth

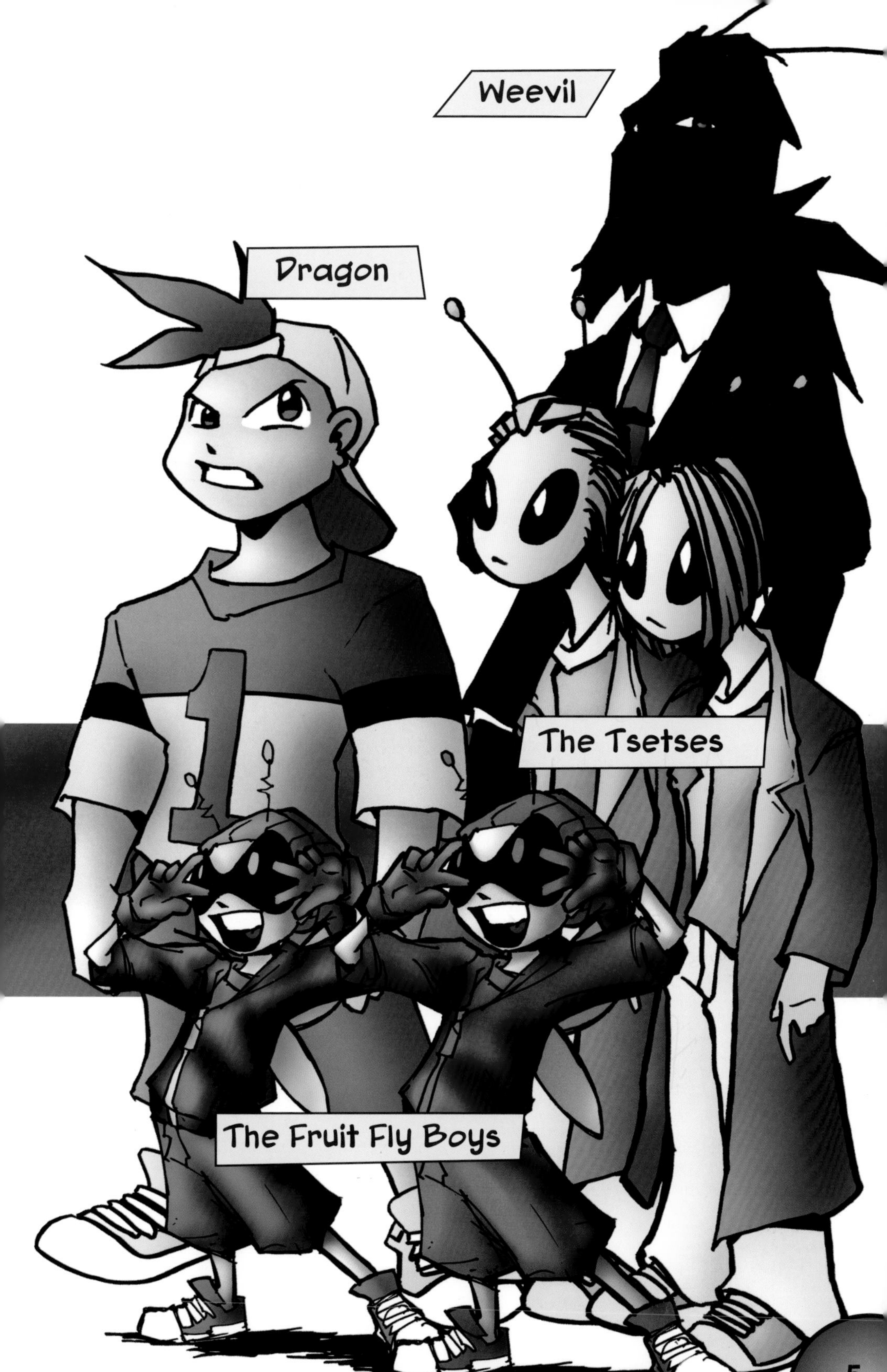
Weevil
Dragon
The Tsetses
The Fruit Fly Boys

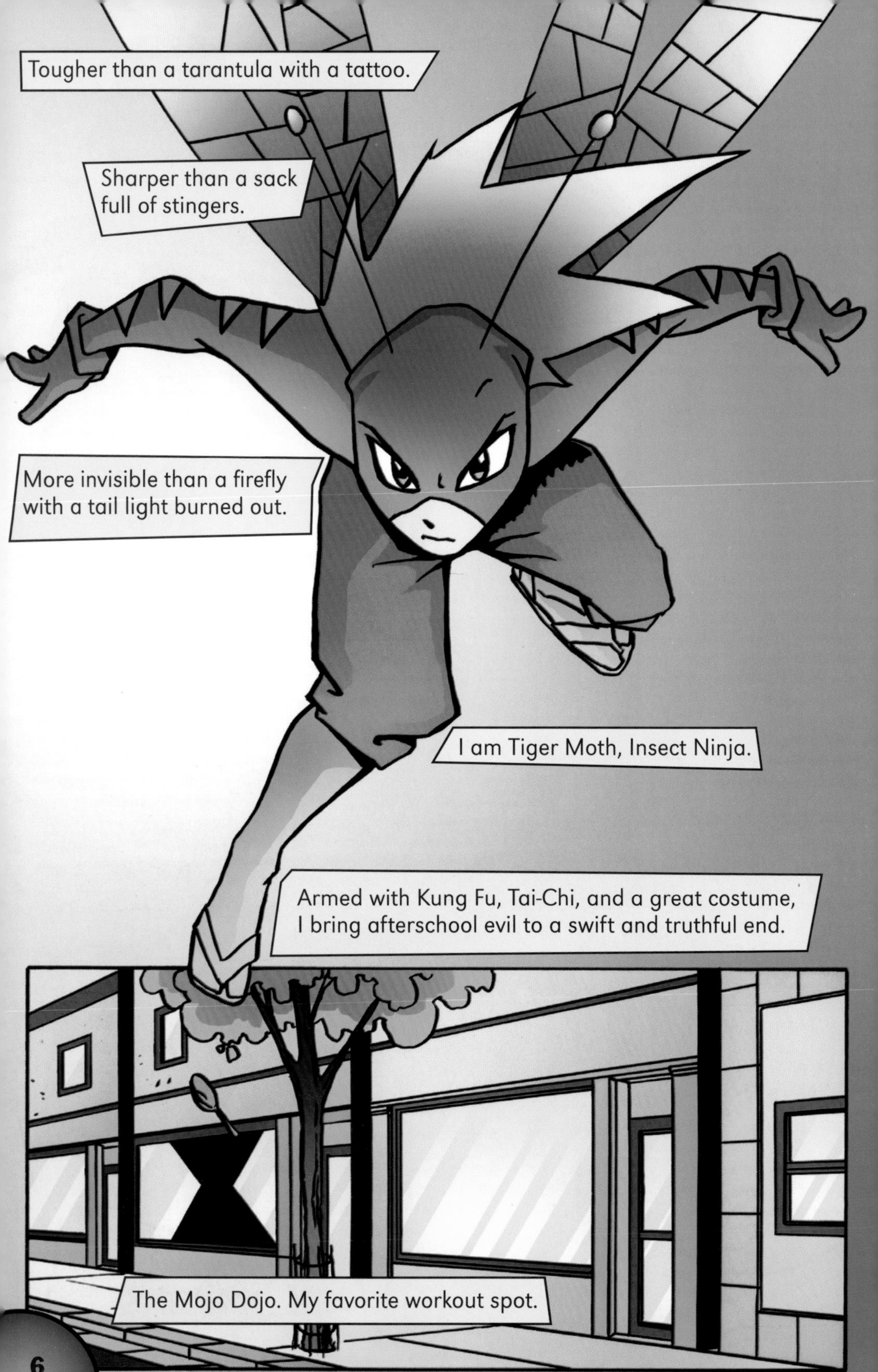
Tougher than a tarantula with a tattoo.
Sharper than a sack full of stingers.
More invisible than a firefly with a tail light burned out.
I am Tiger Moth, Insect Ninja.
Armed with Kung Fu, Tai-Chi, and a great costume, I bring afterschool evil to a swift and truthful end.
The Mojo Dojo. My favorite workout spot.

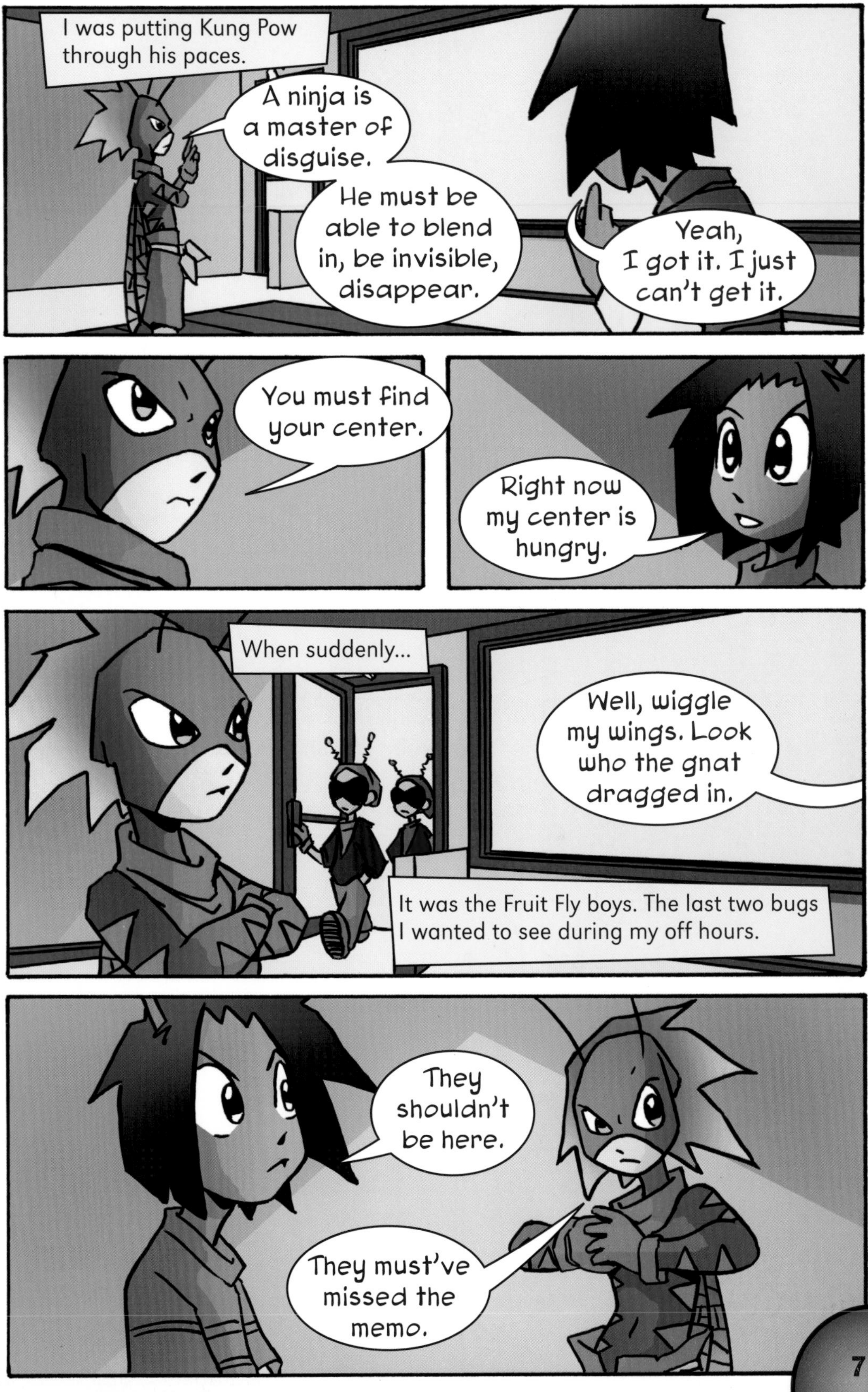
I was putting Kung Pow through his paces.
A ninja is a master of disguise.
He must be able to blend in, be invisible, disappear.
Yeah, I got it. I just can't get it.
You must find your center.
Right now my center is hungry.
When suddenly...
Well, wiggle my wings. Look who the gnat dragged in.
It was the Fruit Fly boys. The last two bugs I wanted to see during my off hours.
They shouldn't be here.
They must've missed the memo.

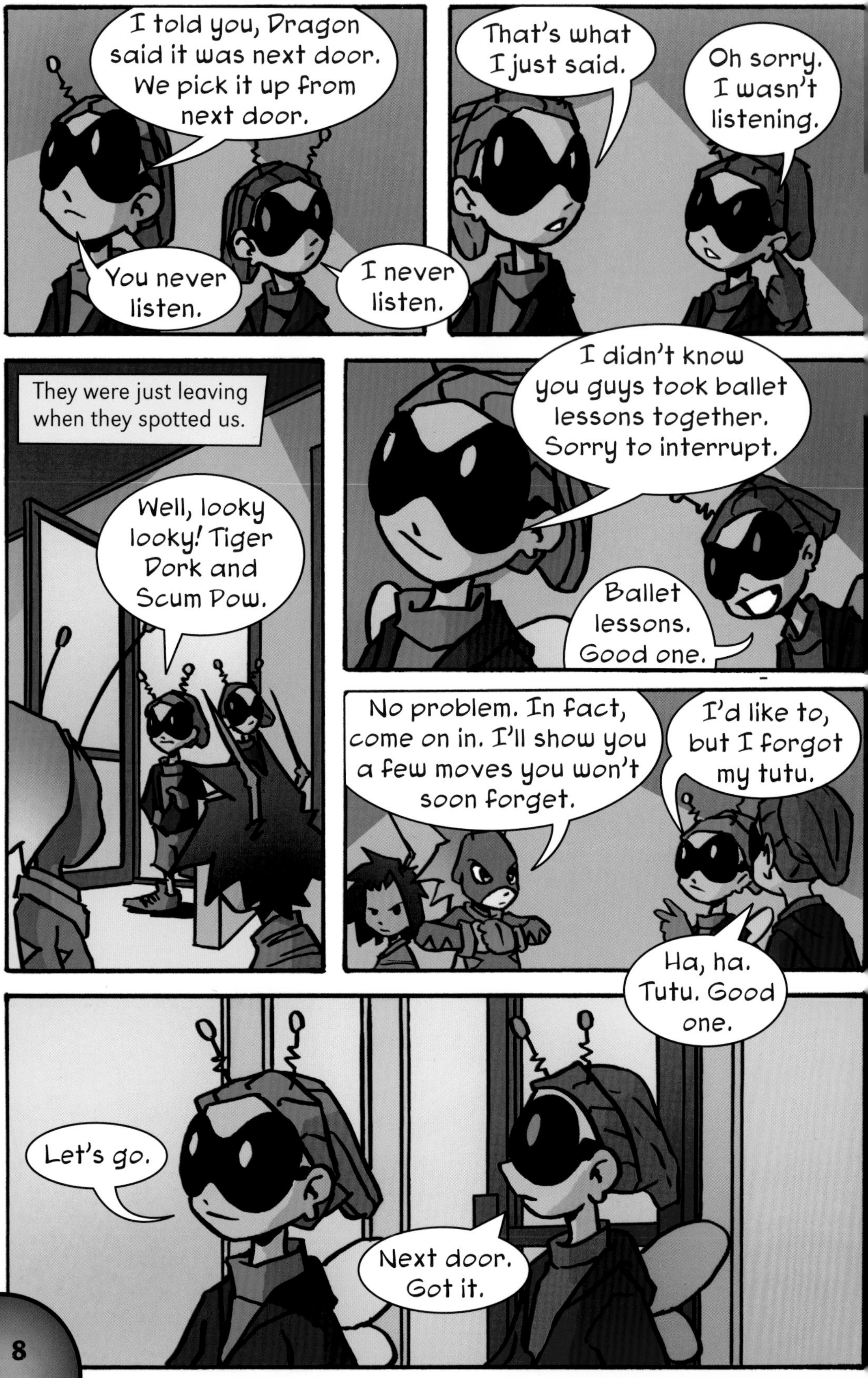
I told you, Dragon said it was next door. We pick it up from next door.
You never listen.
I never listen.
That's what I just said.
Oh sorry. I wasn't listening.
They were just leaving when they spotted us.
Well, looky looky! Tiger Dork and Scum Pow.
I didn't know you guys took ballet lessons together. Sorry to interrupt.
Ballet lessons. Good one.
No problem. In fact, come on in. I'll show you a few moves you won't soon forget.
I'd like to, but I forgot my tutu.
Ha, ha. Tutu. Good one.
Let's go.
Next door. Got it.

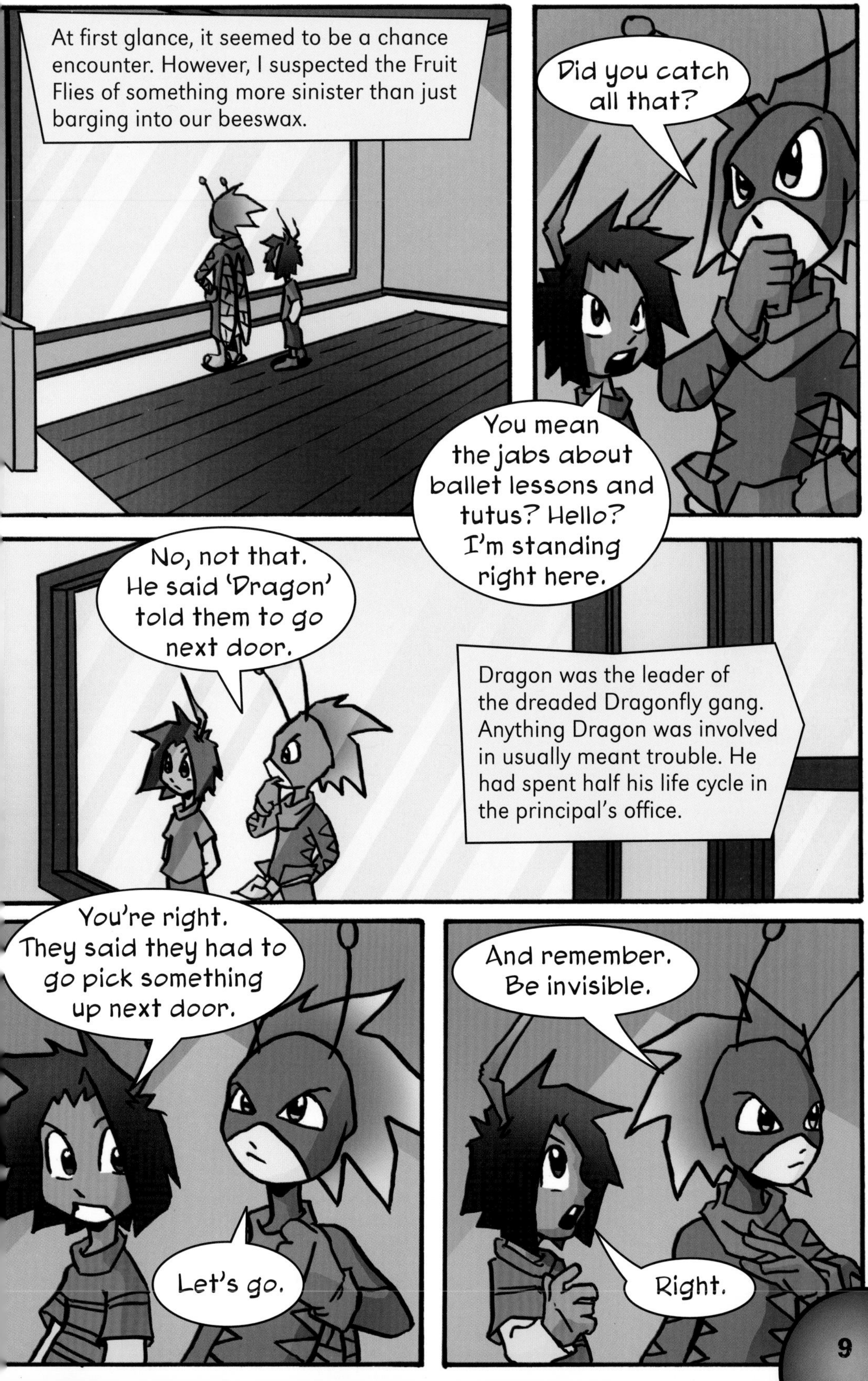
At first glance, it seemed to be a chance encounter. However, I suspected the Fruit Flies of something more sinister than just barging into our beeswax.
Did you catch all that?
You mean the jabs about ballet lessons and tutus? Hello? I'm standing right here.
No, not that. He said 'Dragon' told them to go next door.
Dragon was the leader of the dreaded Dragonfly gang. Anything Dragon was involved in usually meant trouble. He had spent half his life cycle in the principal's office.
You're right. They said they had to go pick something up next door.
Let's go.
And remember. Be invisible.
Right.

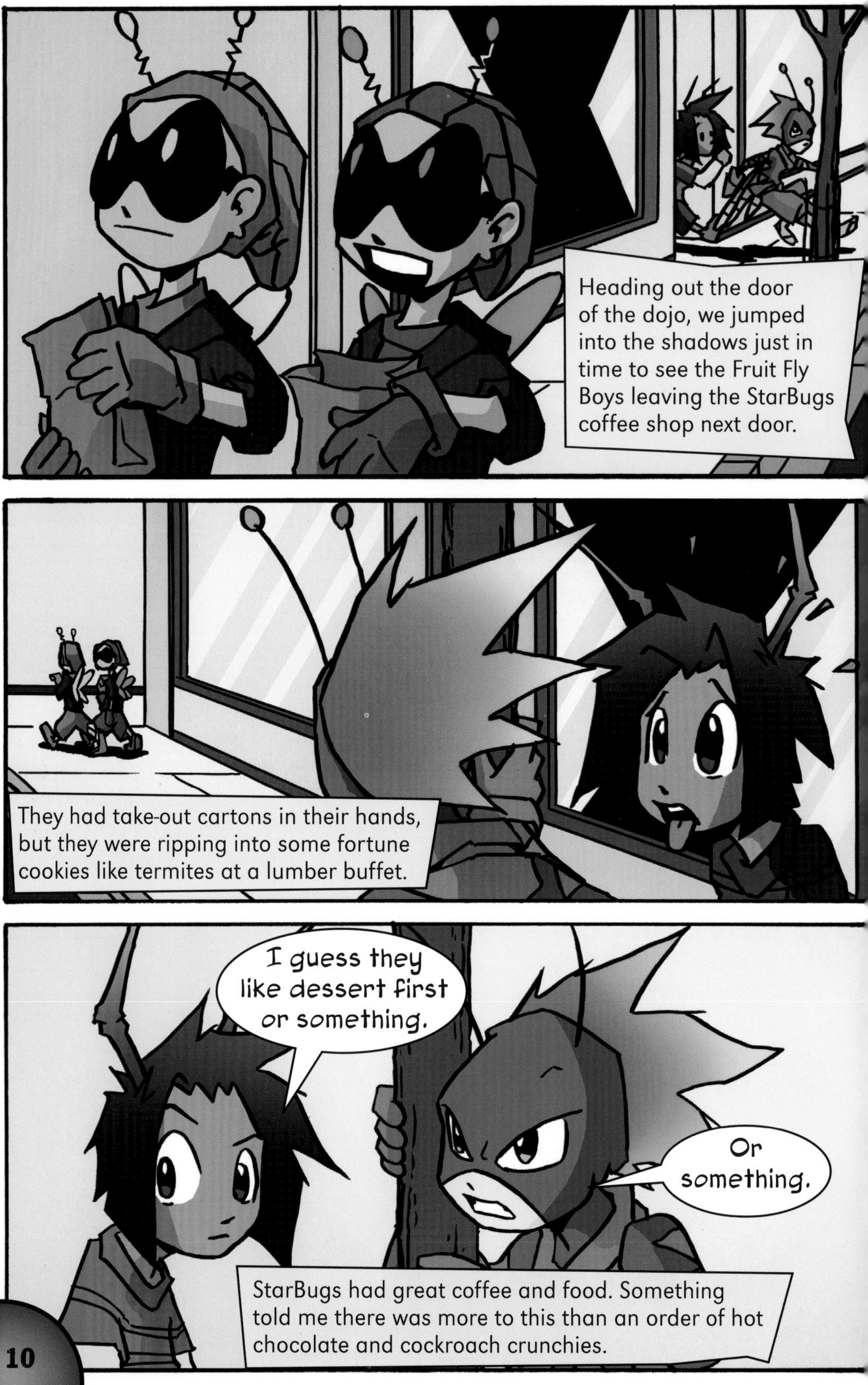
Heading out the door of the dojo, we jumped into the shadows just in time to see the Fruit Fly Boys leaving the StarBugs coffee shop next door.
They had take-out cartons in their hands, but they were ripping into some fortune cookies like termites at a lumber buffet.
I guess they like dessert first or something.
Or something.
StarBugs had great coffee and food. Something told me there was more to this than an order of hot chocolate and cockroach crunchies.

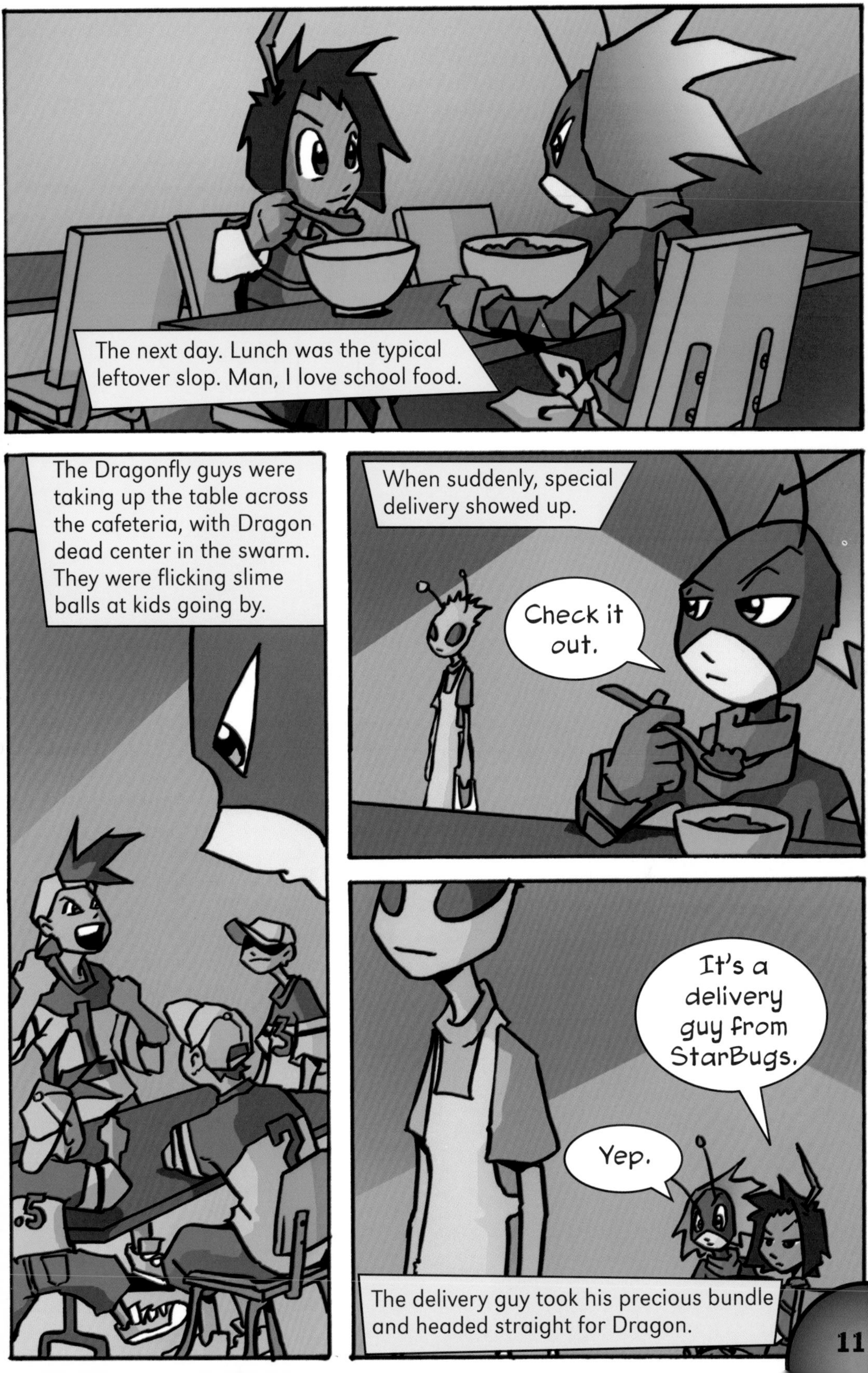

The next day. Lunch was the typical leftover slop. Man, I love school food.
The Dragonfly guys were taking up the table across the cafeteria, with Dragon dead center in the swarm. They were flicking slime balls at kids going by.
When suddenly, special delivery showed up.
Check it out.
It's a delivery guy from StarBugs.
Yep.
The delivery guy took his precious bundle and headed straight for Dragon.

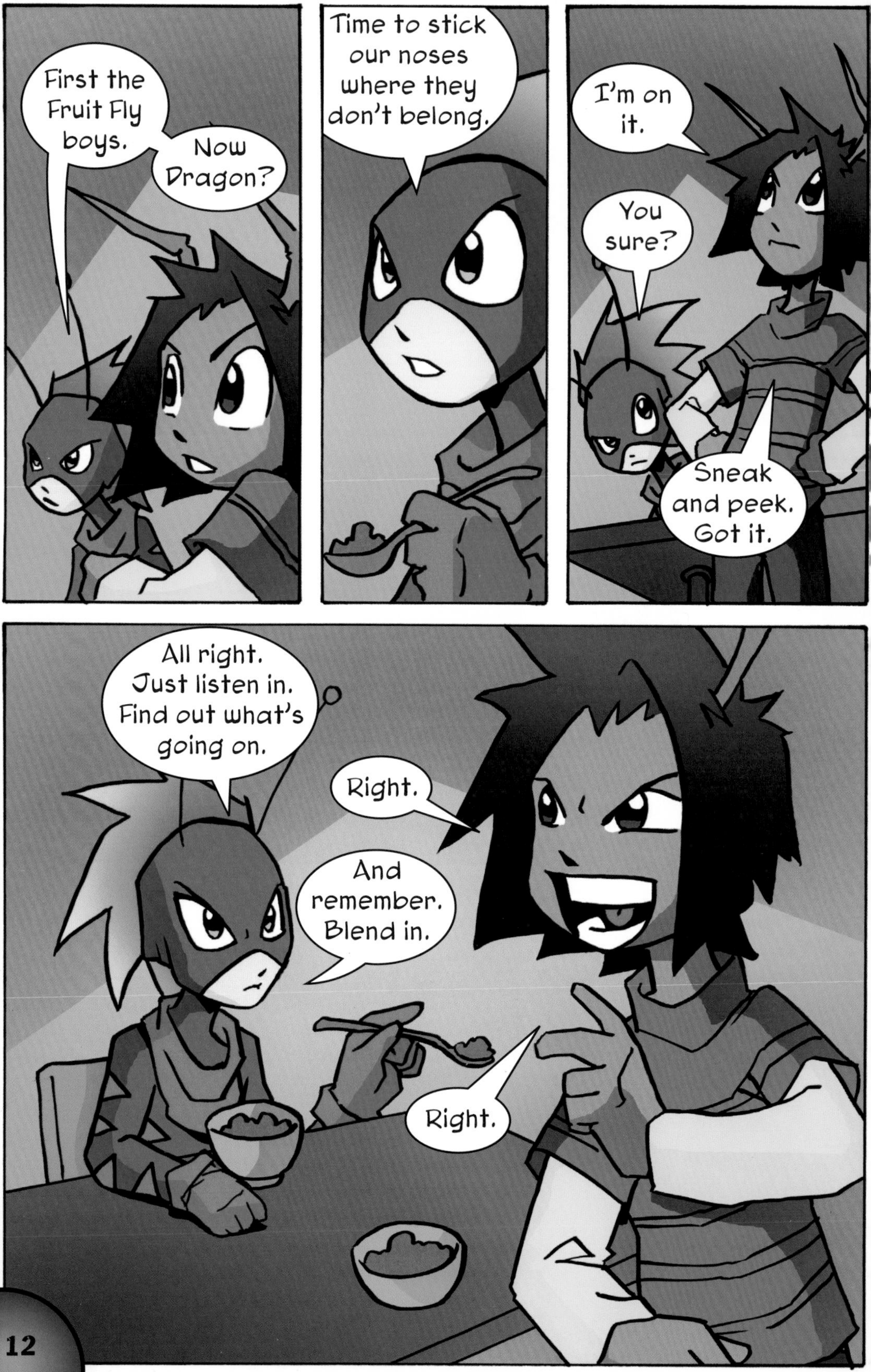
First the Fruit Fly boys.
Now Dragon?
Time to stick our noses where they don't belong.
I'm on it.
You sure?
Sneak and peek. Got it.
All right. Just listen in. Find out what's going on.
Right.
And remember. Blend in.
Right.

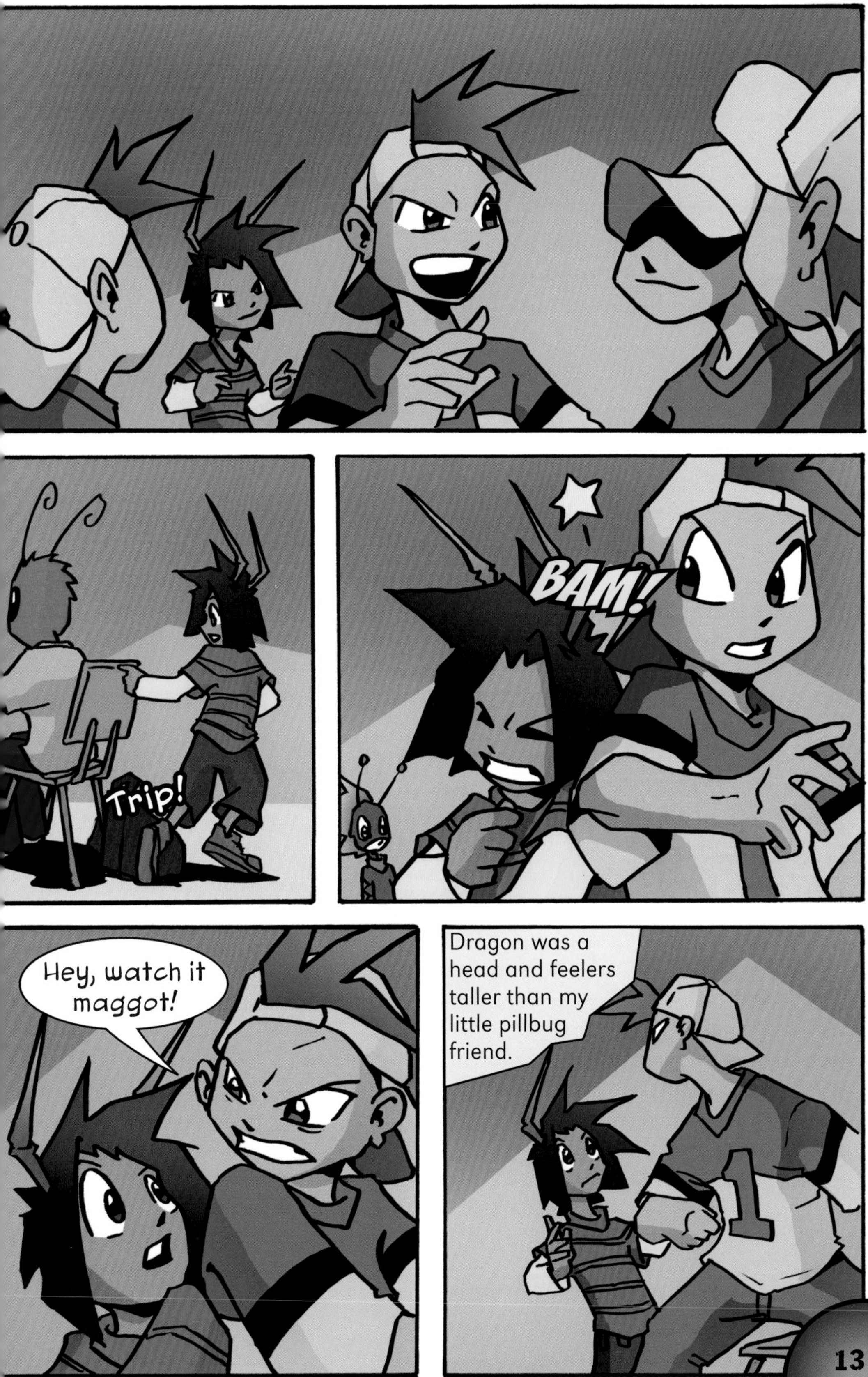
Trip!
BAM!
Hey, watch it maggot!
Dragon was a head and feelers taller than my little pillbug friend.

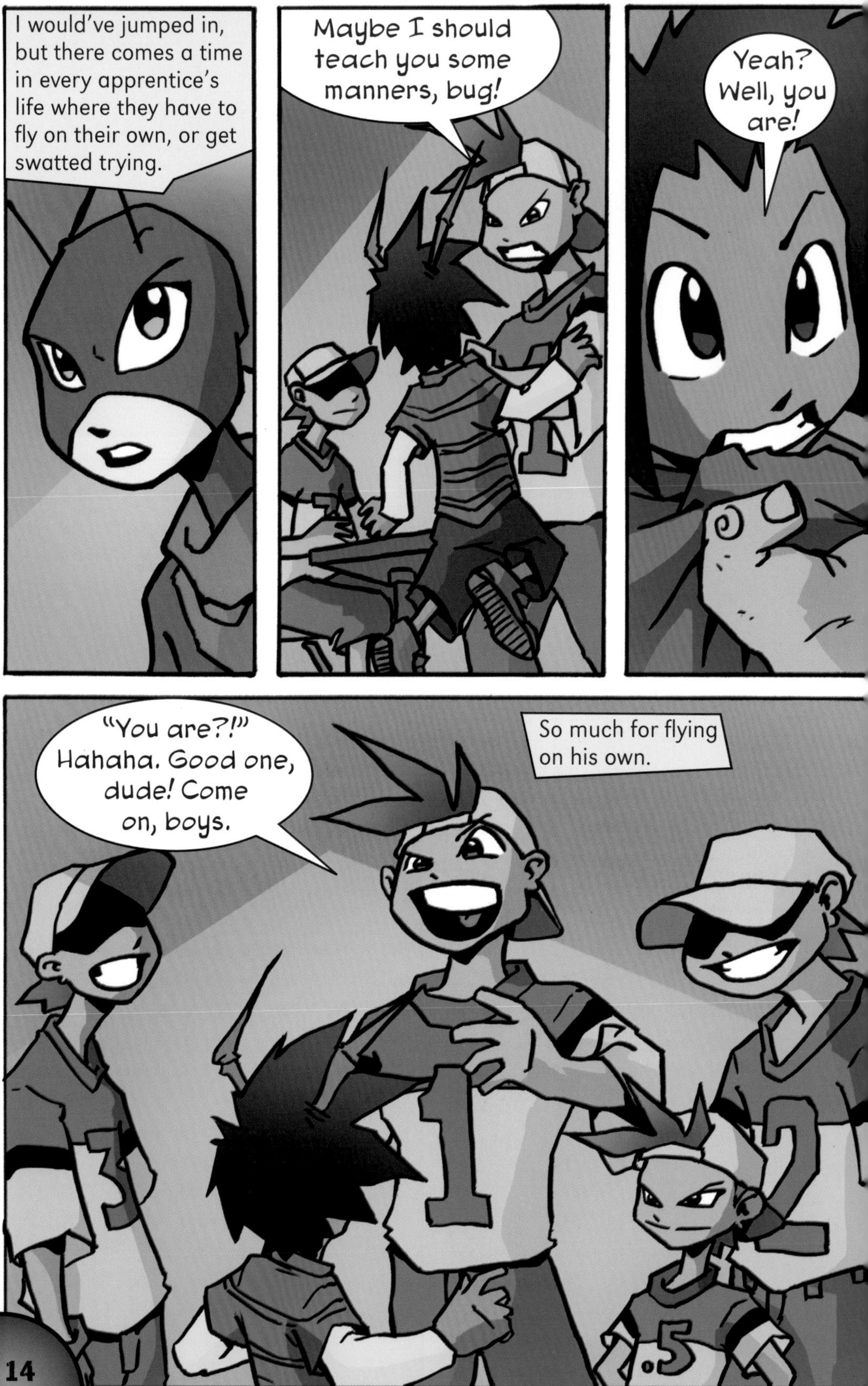
I would've jumped in, but there comes a time in every apprentice's life where they have to fly on their own, or get swatted trying.
Maybe I should teach you some manners, bug!
Yeah? Well, you are!
"You are?!" Hahaha. Good one, dude! Come on, boys.
So much for flying on his own.

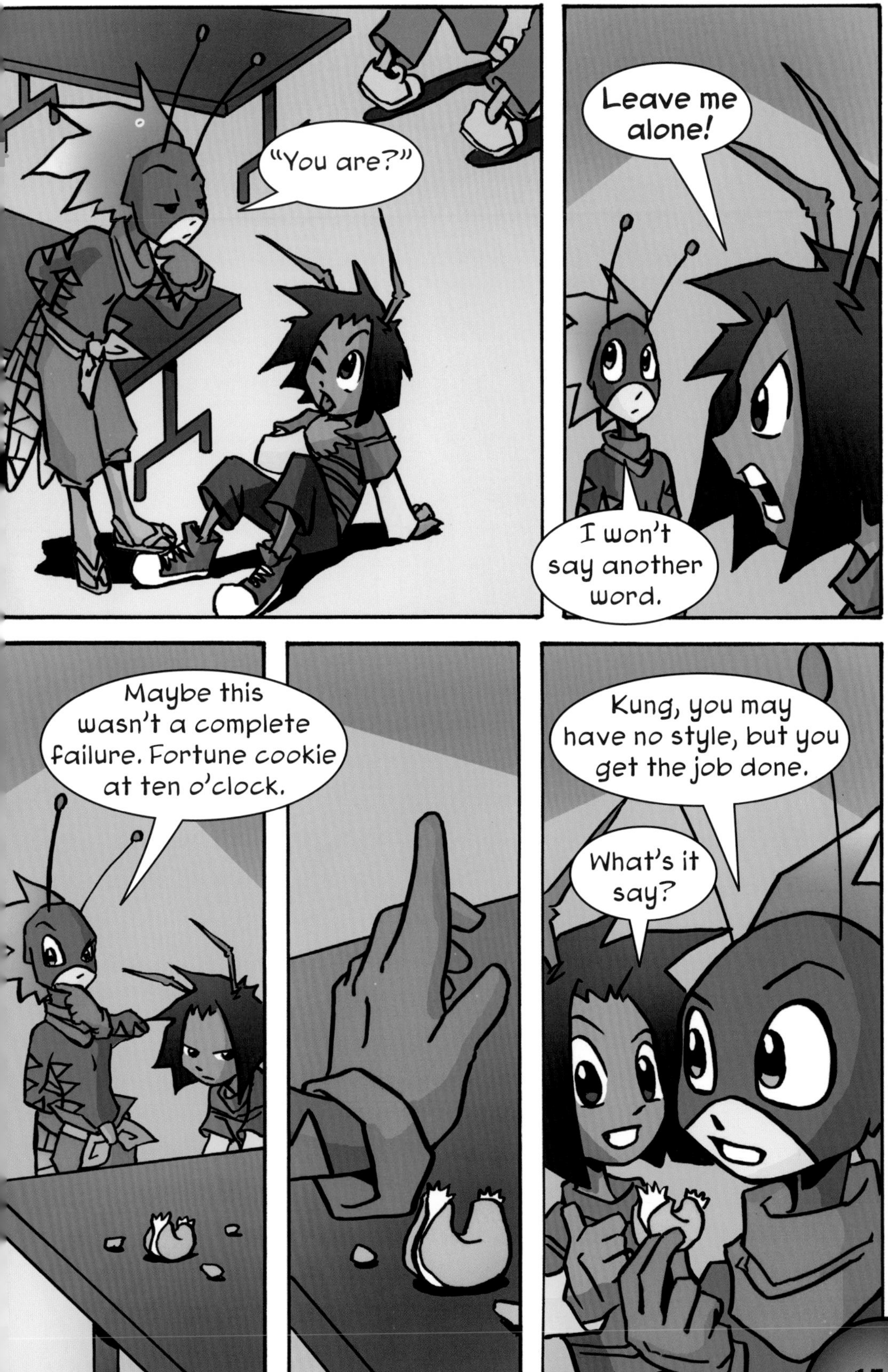
"You are?"
Leave me alone!
I won't say another word.
Maybe this wasn't a complete failure. Fortune cookie at ten o'clock.
Kung, you may have no style, but you get the job done.
What's it say?

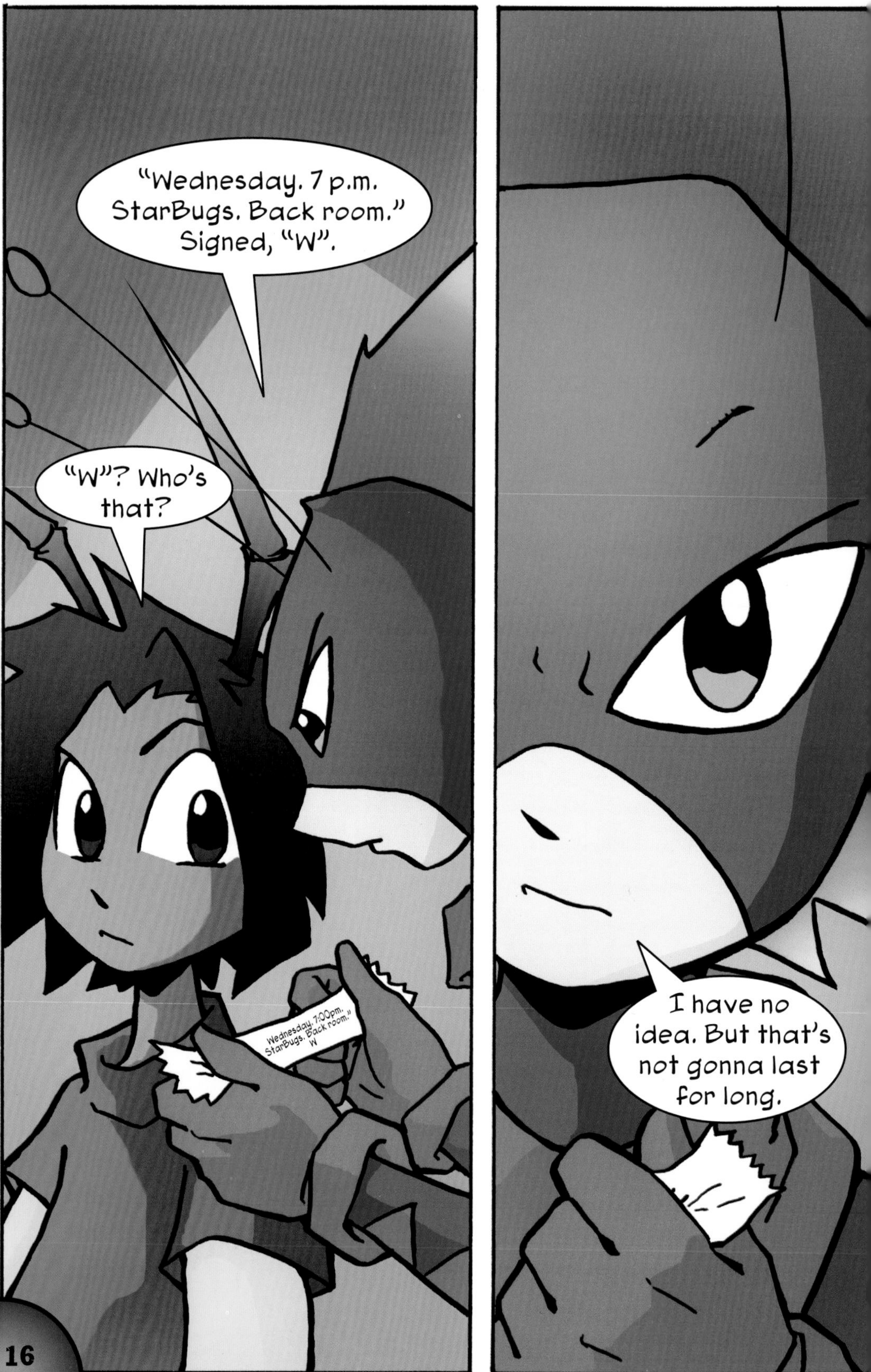
"Wednesday. 7 p.m. StarBugs. Back room." Signed, "W".
"W"? Who's that?
Wednesday. 7:00pm. StarBugs. Back room." W
I have no idea. But that's not gonna last for long.

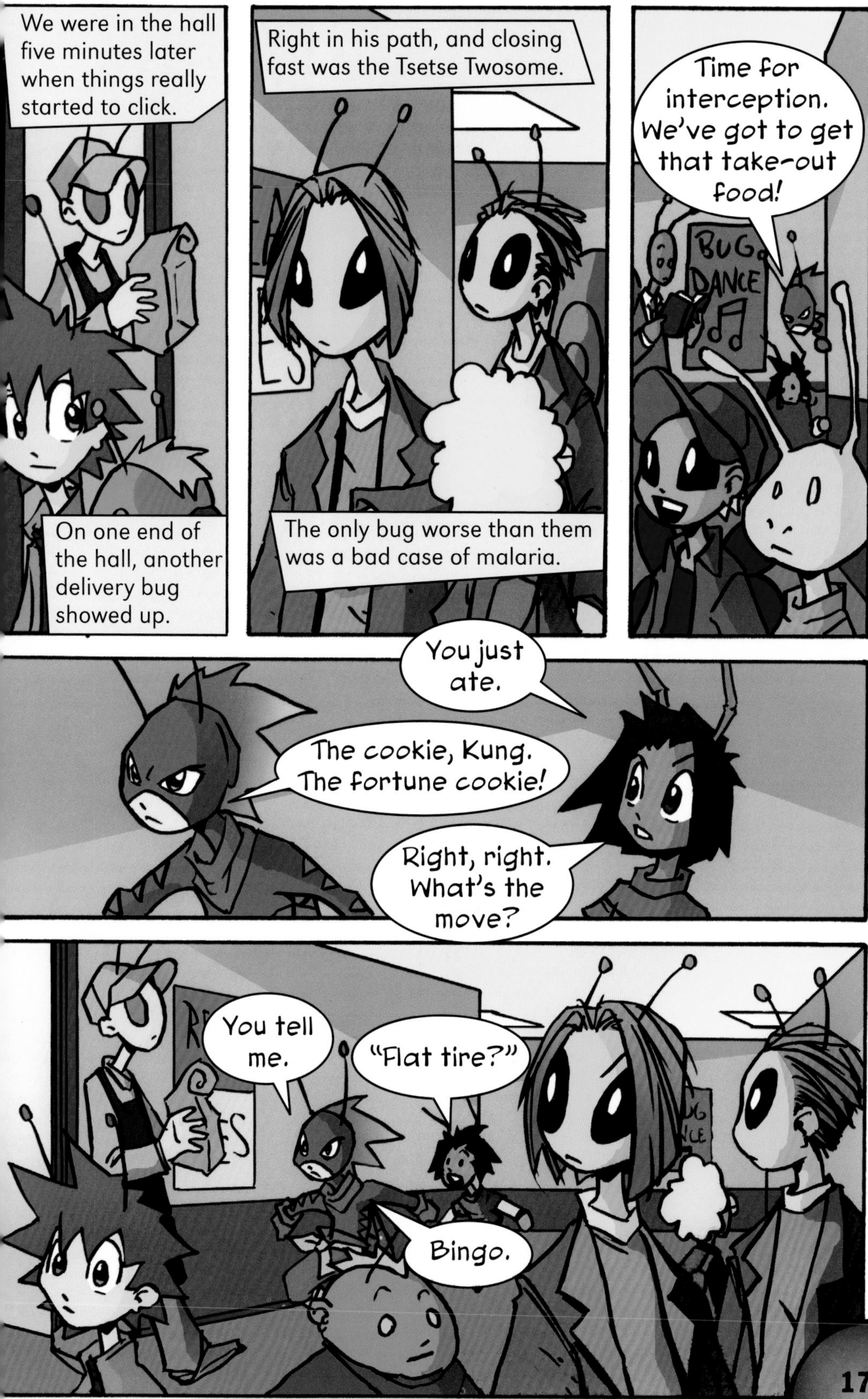
We were in the hall five minutes later when things really started to click.
On one end of the hall, another delivery bug showed up.
Right in his path, and closing fast was the Tsetse Twosome.
The only bug worse than them was a bad case of malaria.
Time for interception. We've got to get that take-out food!
BUG DANCE
You just ate.
The cookie, Kung. The fortune cookie!
Right, right. What's the move?
You tell me.
"Flat tire?"
Bingo.

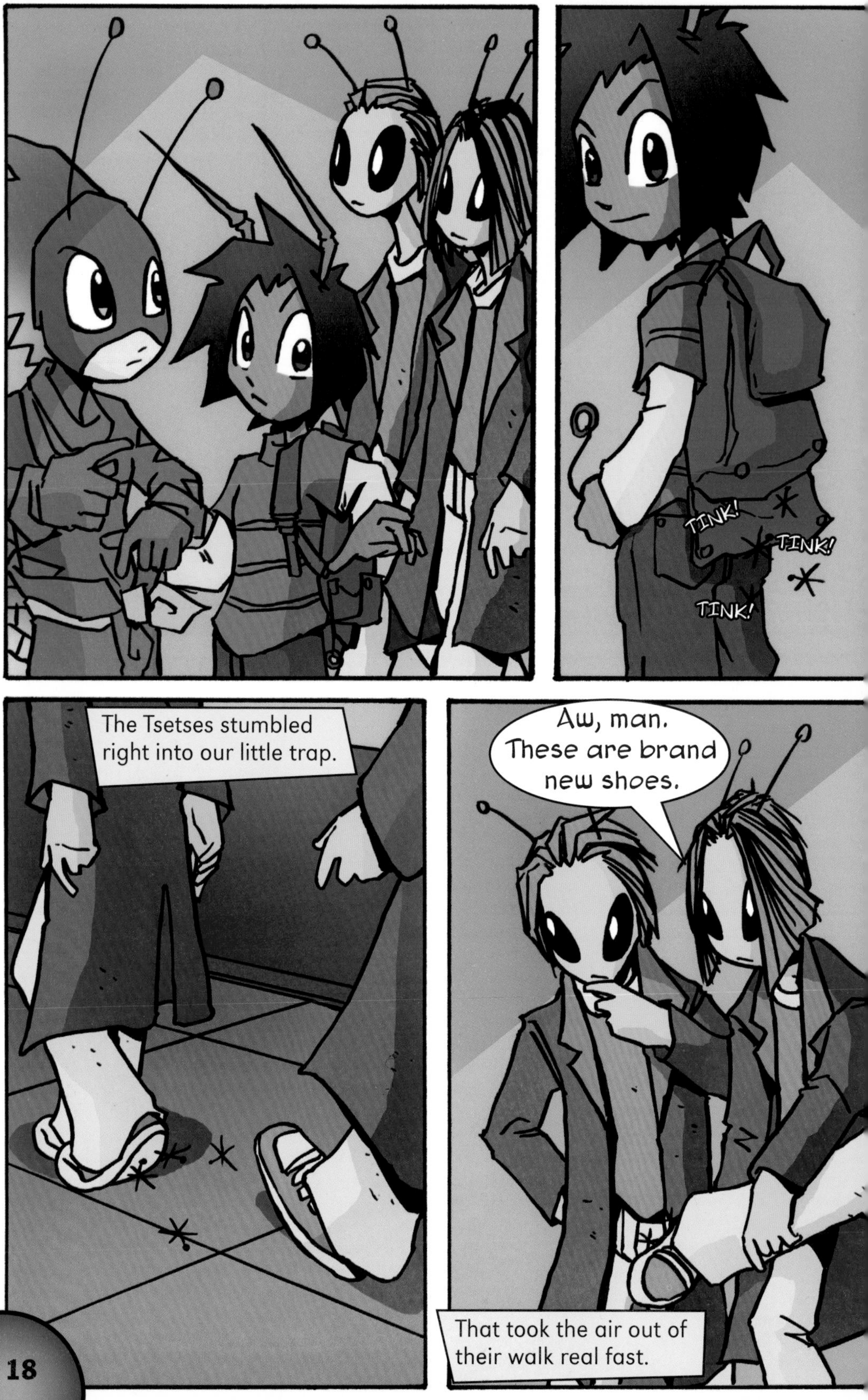
TINK!
TINK!
TINK!
The Tsetses stumbled right into our little trap.
Aw, man. These are brand new shoes.
That took the air out of their walk real fast.

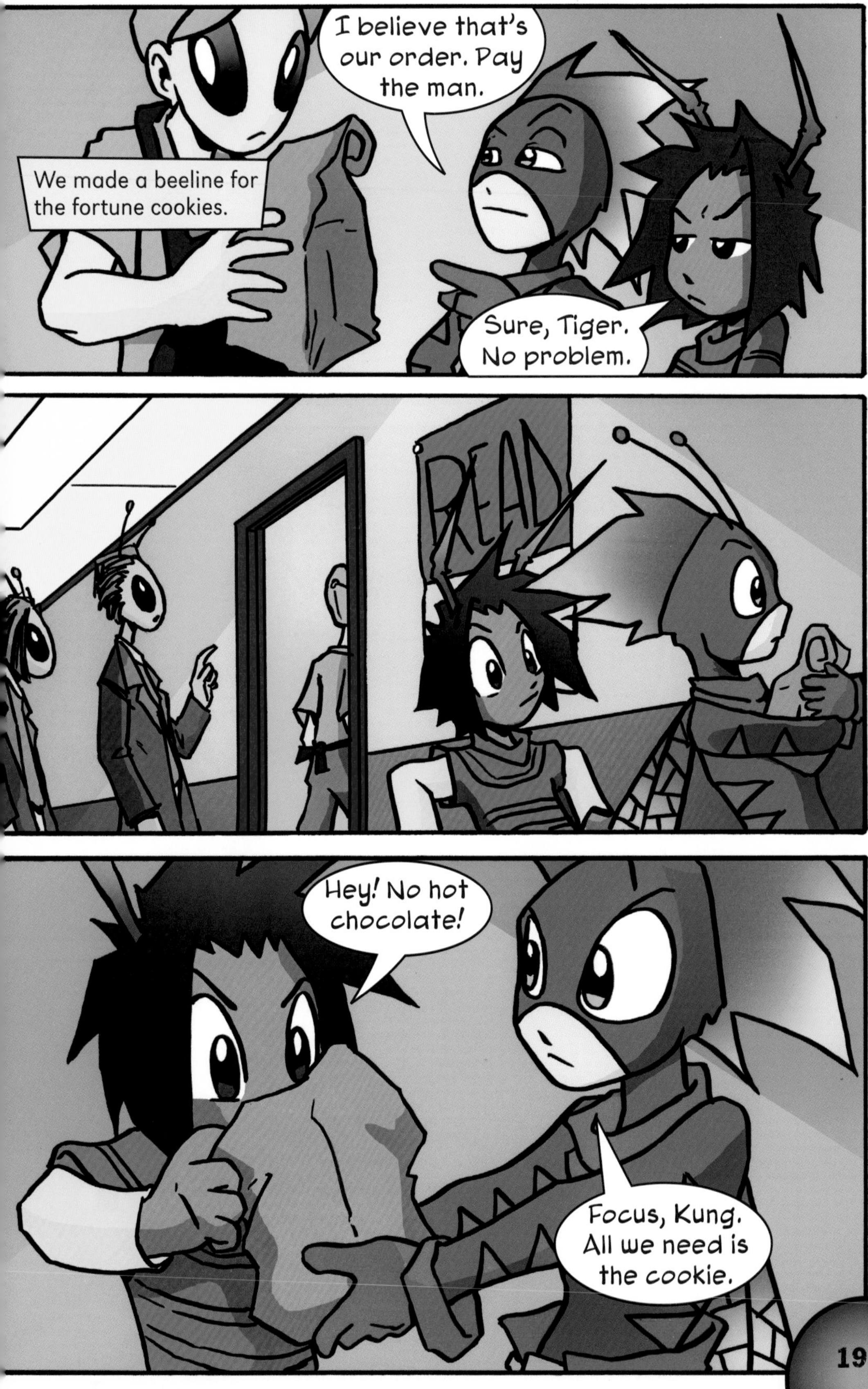
I believe that's our order. Pay the man.
We made a beeline for the fortune cookies.
Sure, Tiger. No problem.
READ
Hey! No hot chocolate!
Focus, Kung. All we need is the cookie.

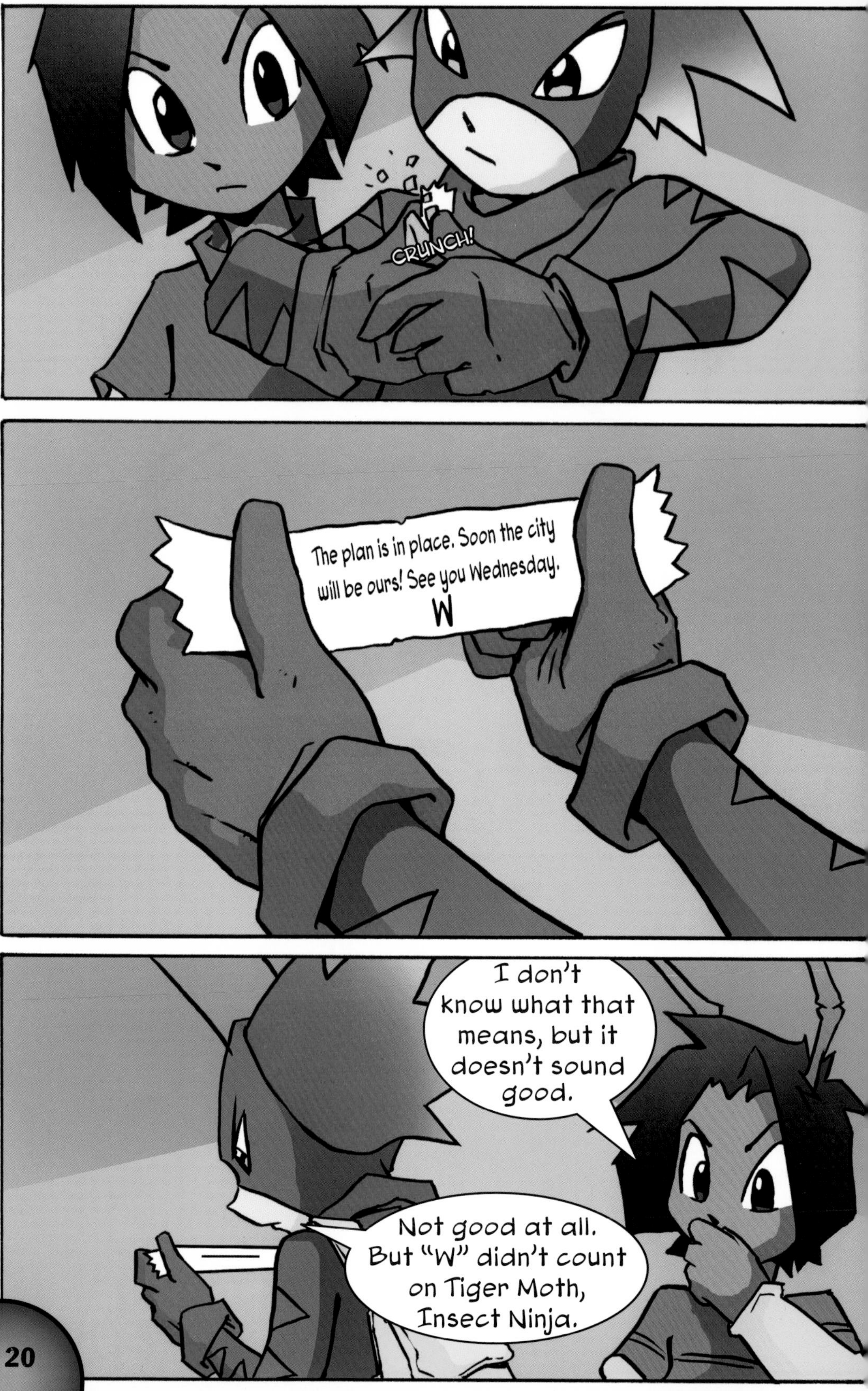
CRUNCH!
The plan is in place. Soon the city will be ours! See you Wednesday.
W
I don't know what that means, but it doesn't sound good.
Not good at all. But "W" didn't count on Tiger Moth, Insect Ninja.

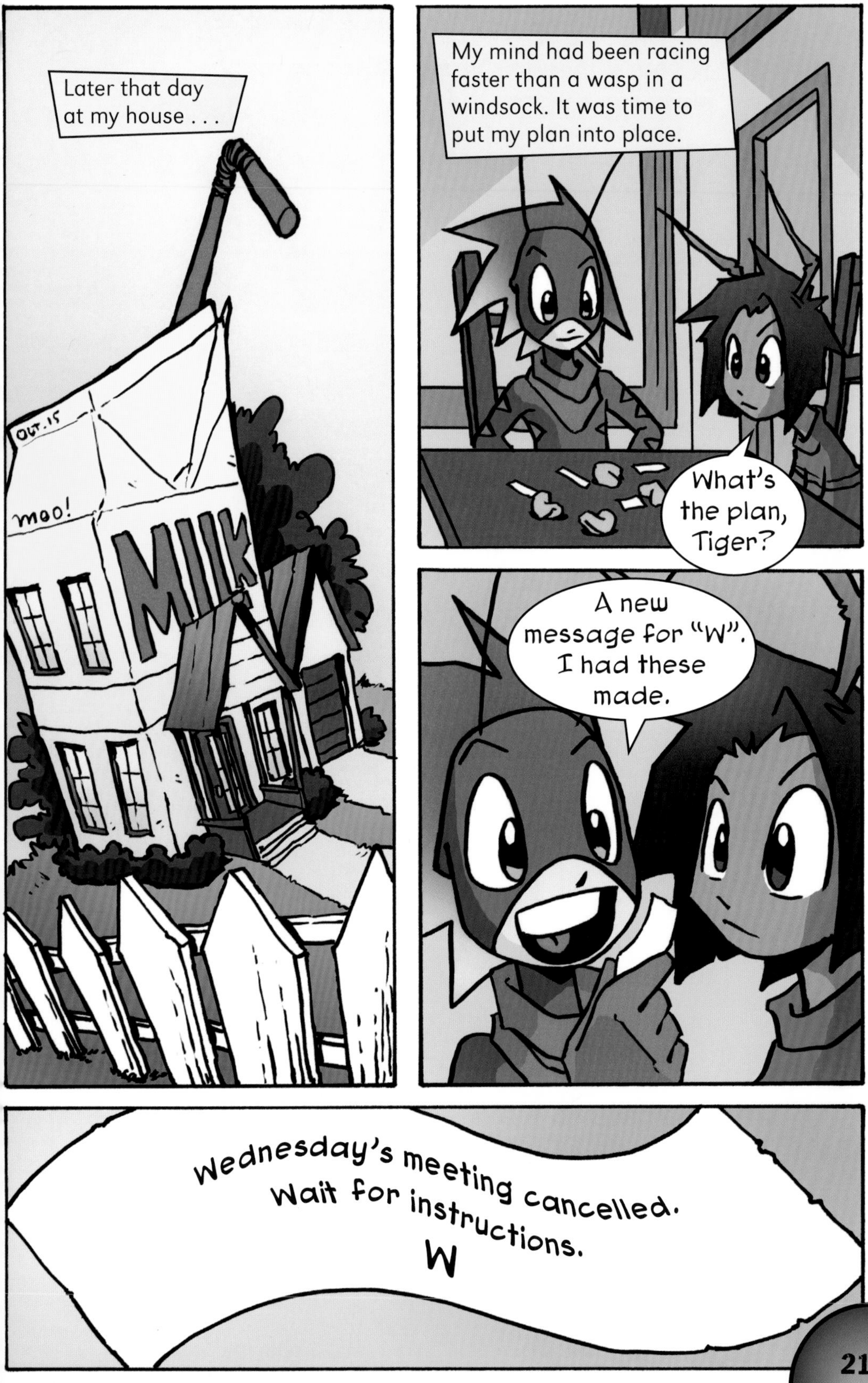
Later that day at my house . . .
OCT. 15
moo!
MILK
My mind had been racing faster than a wasp in a windsock. It was time to put my plan into place.
What's the plan, Tiger?
A new message for "W". I had these made.
Wednesday's meeting cancelled.
Wait for instructions.
W

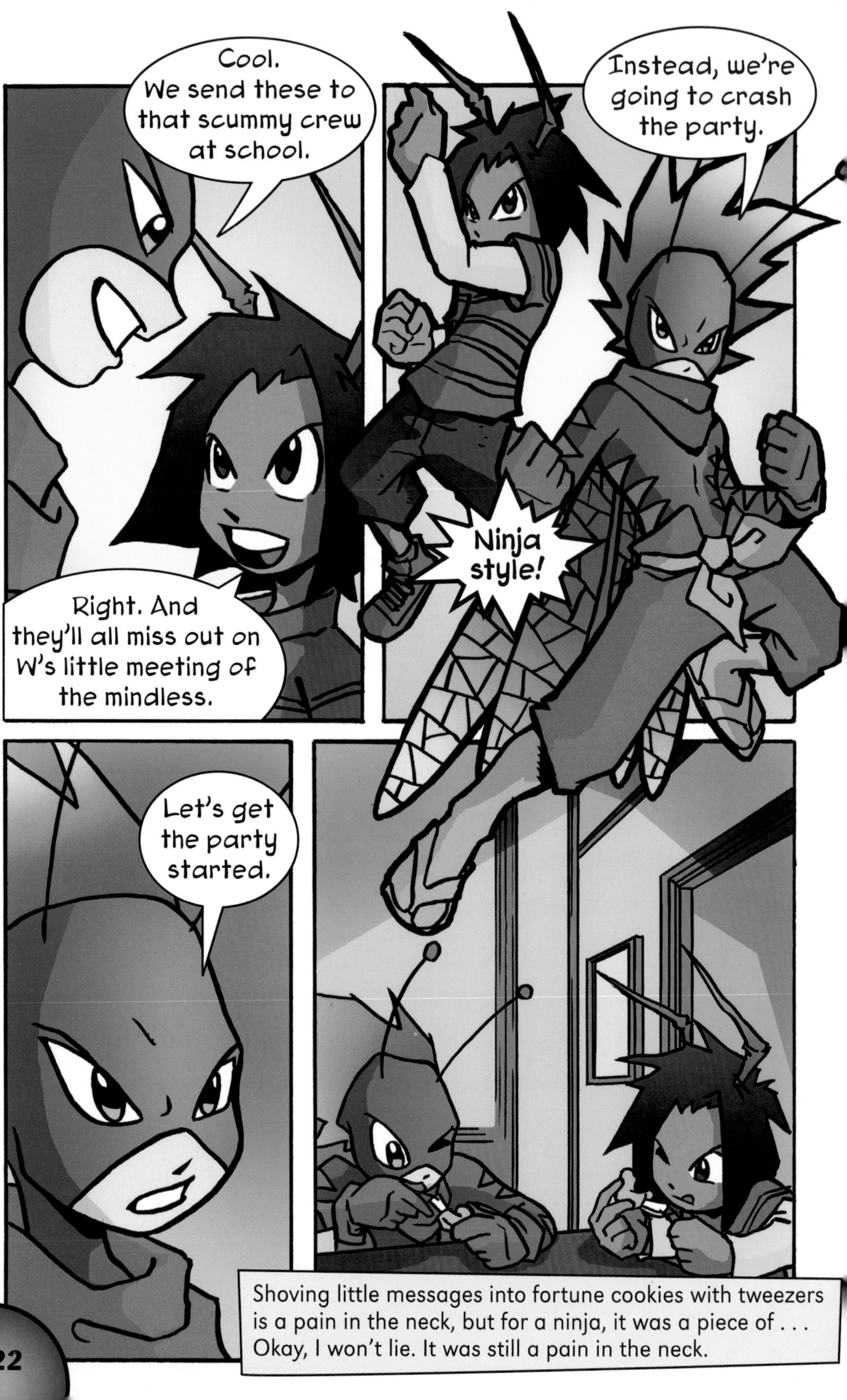
Cool.
We send these to that scummy crew at school.
Right. And they'll all miss out on W's little meeting of the mindless.
Instead, we're going to crash the party.
Ninja style!
Let's get the party started.
Shoving little messages into fortune cookies with tweezers is a pain in the neck, but for a ninja, it was a piece of . . . Okay, I won't lie. It was still a pain in the neck.

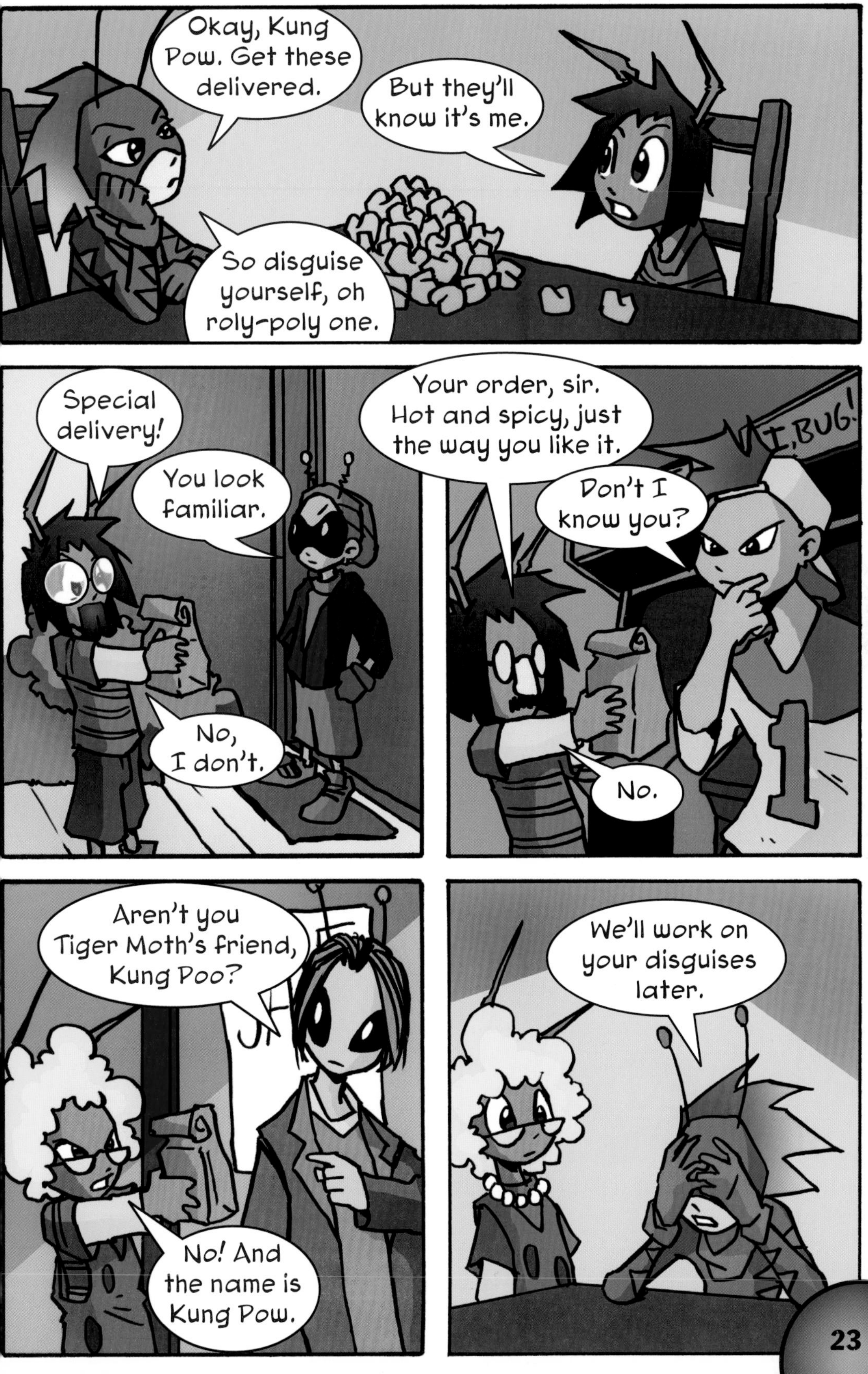
Okay, Kung Pow. Get these delivered.
But they'll know it's me.
So disguise yourself, oh roly-poly one.
Special delivery!
You look familiar.
No, I don't.
Your order, sir. Hot and spicy, just the way you like it.
I, BUG!
Don't I know you?
No.
Aren't you Tiger Moth's friend, Kung Poo?
No! And the name is Kung Pow.
We'll work on your disguises later.

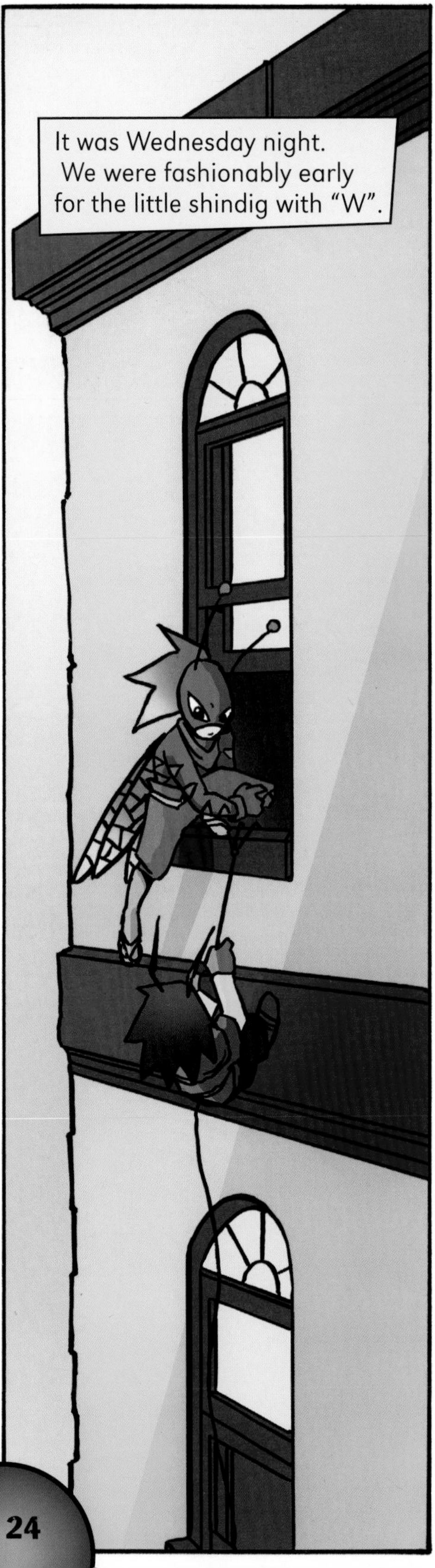
It was Wednesday night. We were fashionably early for the little shindig with "W".

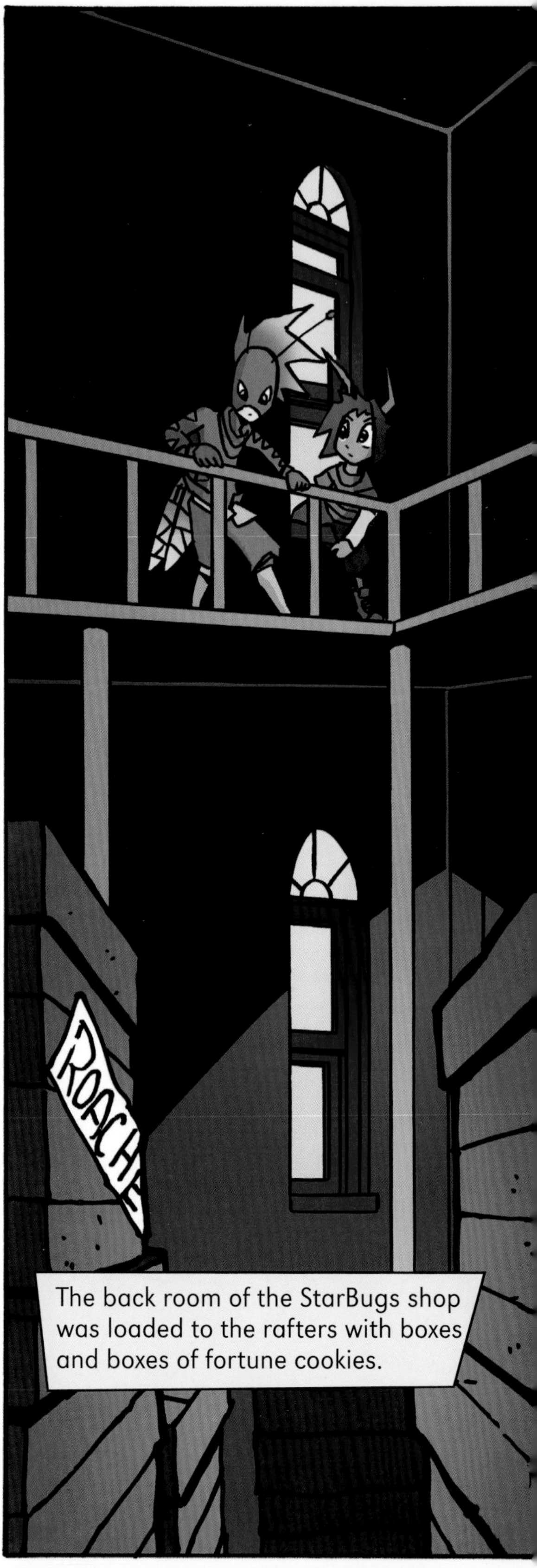
ROACHE
The back room of the StarBugs shop was loaded to the rafters with boxes and boxes of fortune cookies.

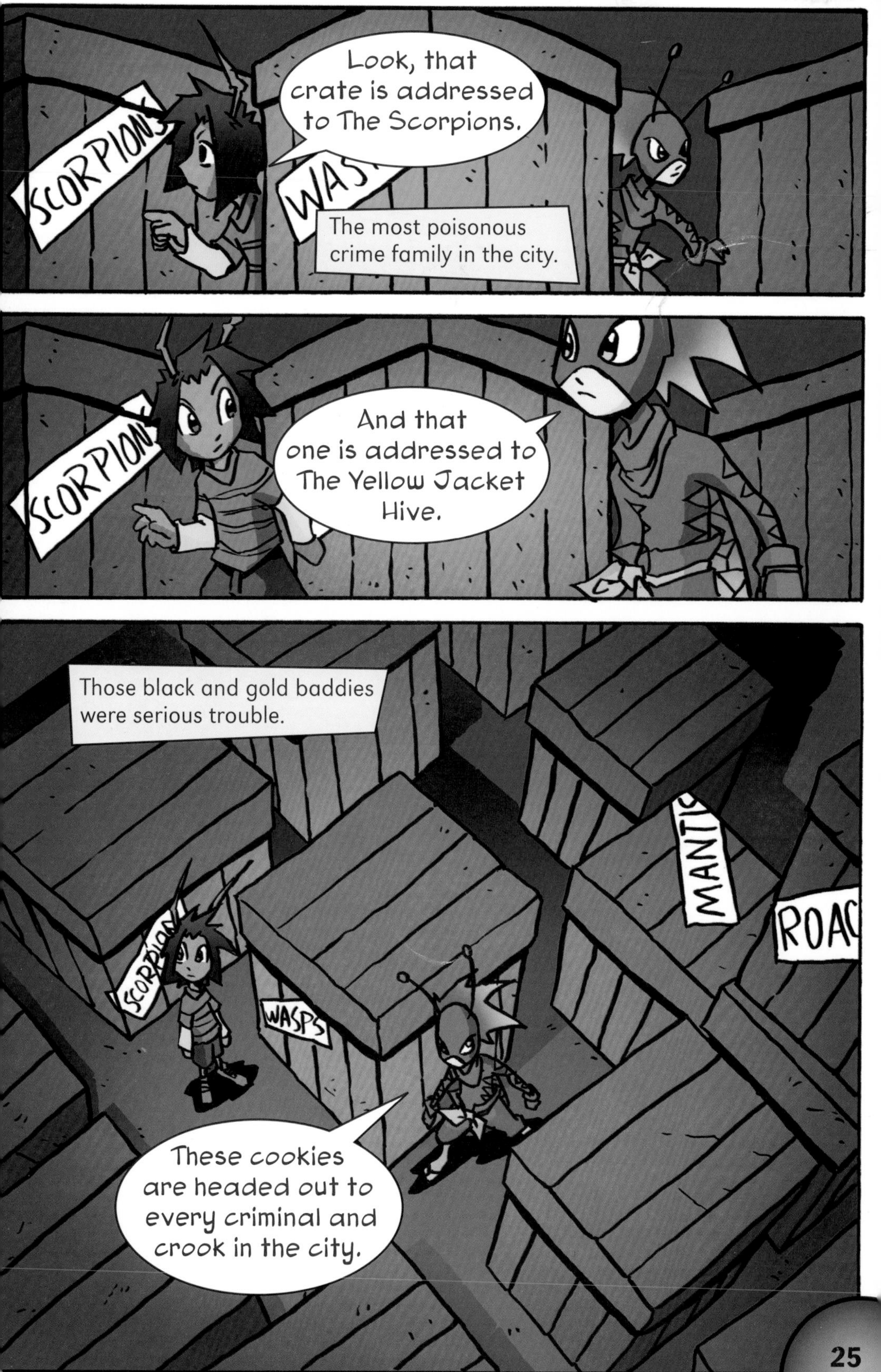
Look, that crate is addressed to The Scorpions.
The most poisonous crime family in the city.
And that one is addressed to The Yellow Jacket Hive.
Those black and gold baddies were serious trouble.
These cookies are headed out to every criminal and crook in the city.
SCORPIONS
WASPS
MANTIS
ROAC

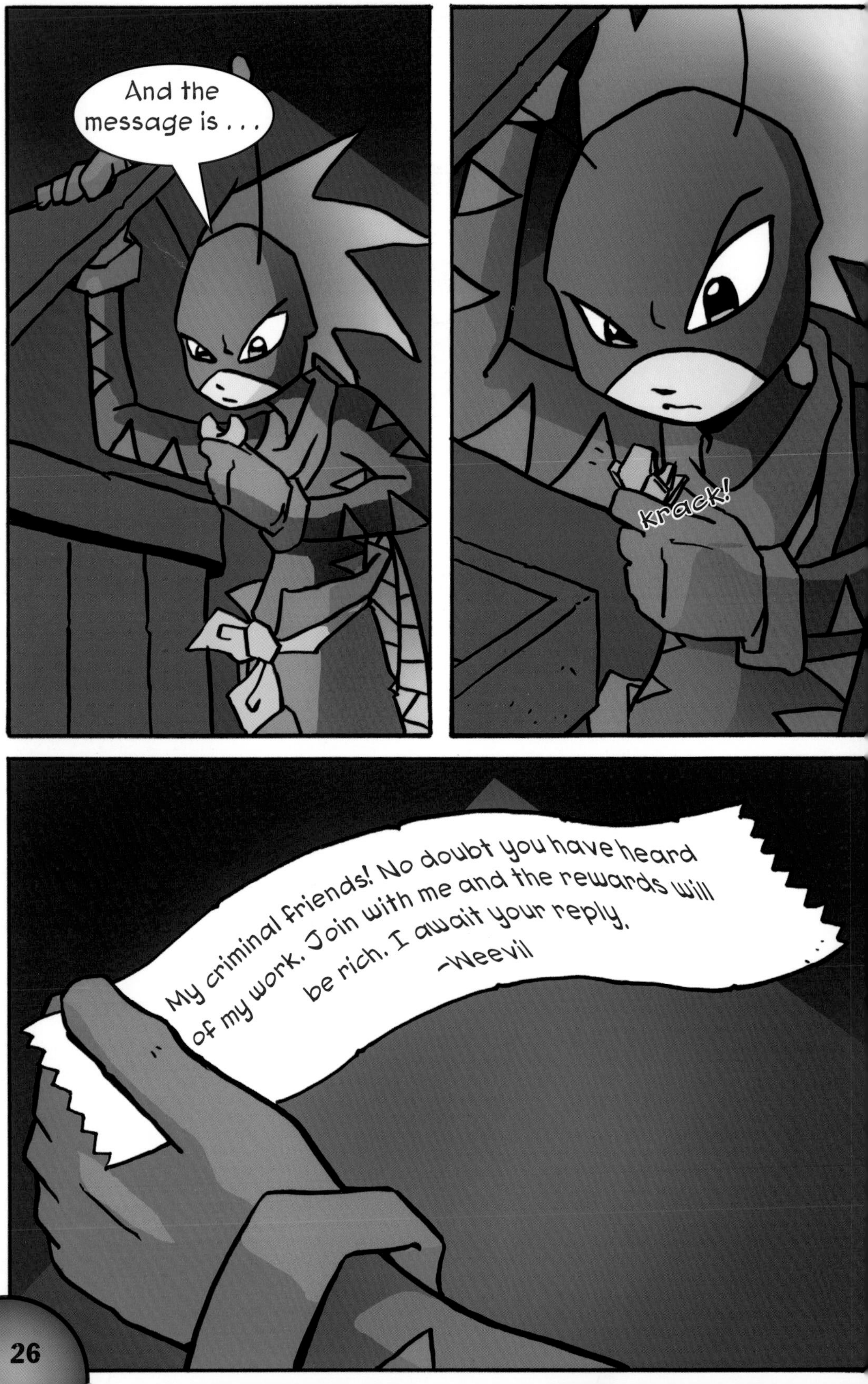
And the message is . . .
krack!
My criminal friends! No doubt you have heard of my work. Join with me and the rewards will be rich. I await your reply.
-Weevil

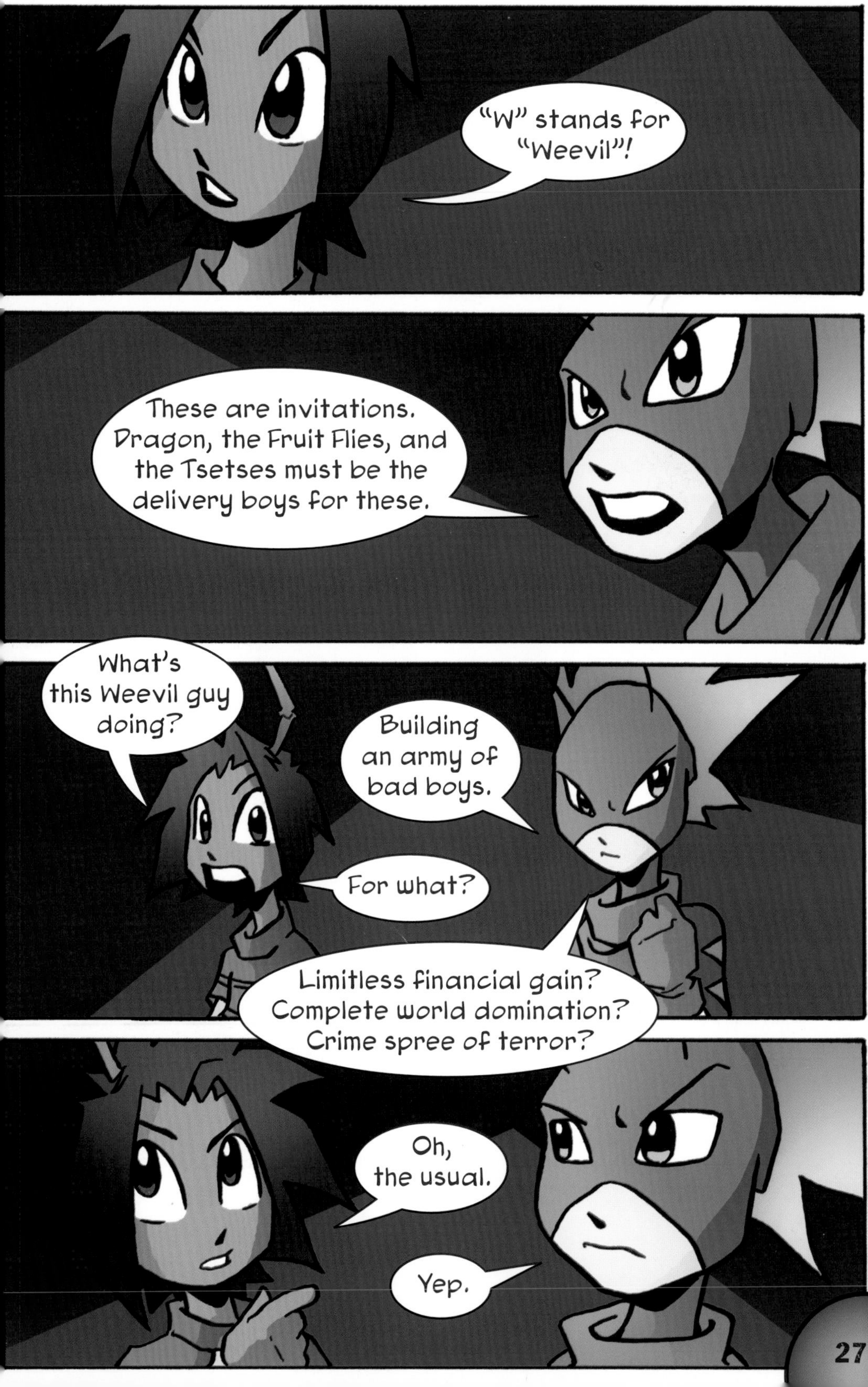
"W" stands for "Weevil"!
These are invitations. Dragon, the Fruit Flies, and the Tsetses must be the delivery boys for these.
What's this Weevil guy doing?
Building an army of bad boys.
For what?
Limitless financial gain? Complete world domination? Crime spree of terror?
Oh, the usual.
Yep.

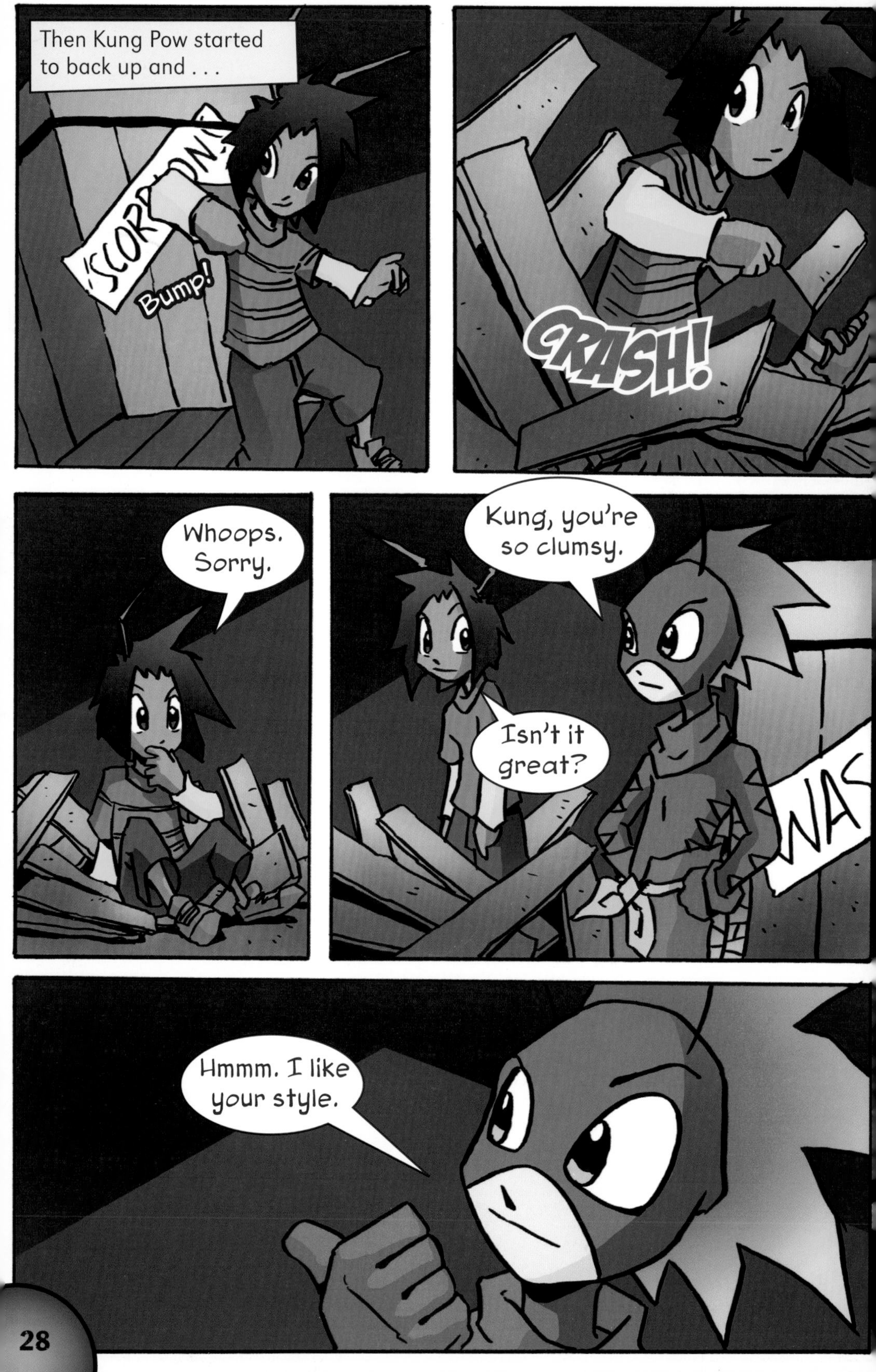
Then Kung Pow started to back up and . . .
SCORPION!
Bump!
CRASH!
Whoops. Sorry.
Kung, you're so clumsy.
Isn't it great?
WAS
Hmmm. I like your style.

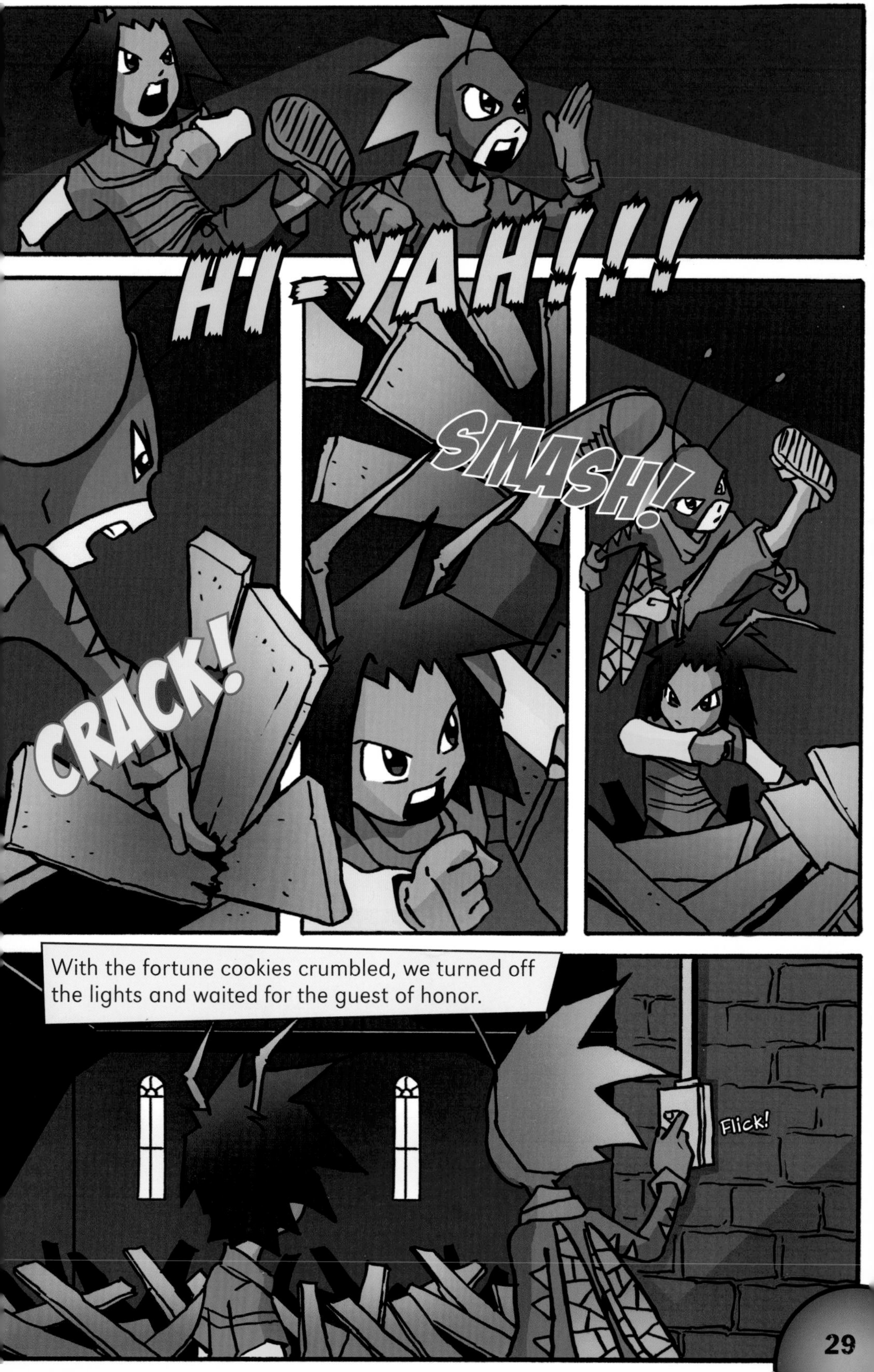
HI-YAH!!!!
CRACK!
SMASH!
With the fortune cookies crumbled, we turned off the lights and waited for the guest of honor.
Flick!

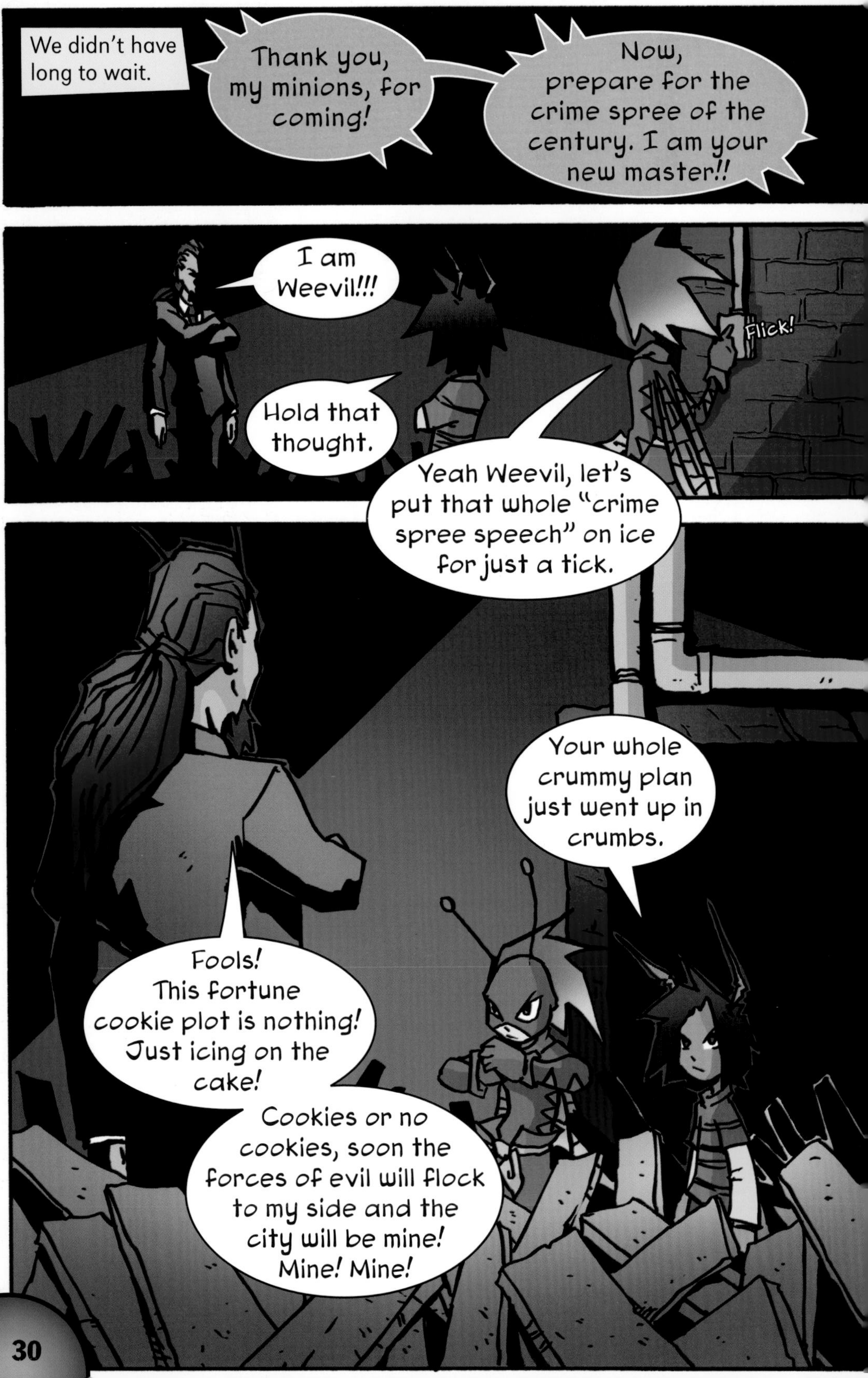
We didn't have long to wait.
Thank you, my minions, for coming!
Now, prepare for the crime spree of the century. I am your new master!!
I am Weevil!!!
Hold that thought.
Flick!
Yeah Weevil, let's put that whole "crime spree speech" on ice for just a tick.
Your whole crummy plan just went up in crumbs.
Fools! This fortune cookie plot is nothing! Just icing on the cake!
Cookies or no cookies, soon the forces of evil will flock to my side and the city will be mine! Mine! Mine!

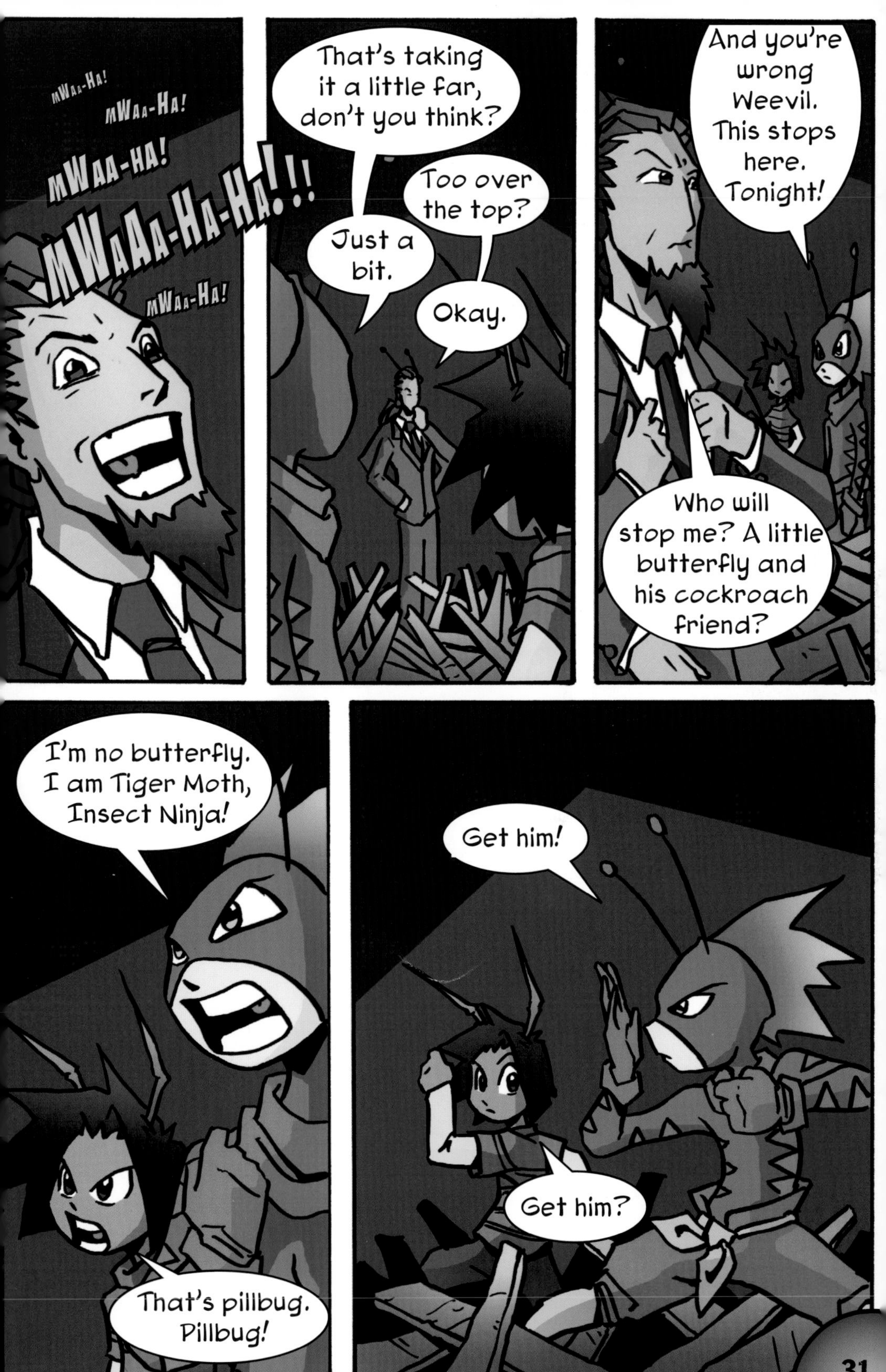
mWAA-HA!
mWAA-HA!
mWAA-HA!
mWAAA-HA-HA!!!
mWAA-HA!
That's taking it a little far, don't you think?
Too over the top?
Just a bit.
Okay.
And you're wrong Weevil. This stops here. Tonight!
Who will stop me? A little butterfly and his cockroach friend?
I'm no butterfly. I am Tiger Moth, Insect Ninja!
That's pillbug. Pillbug!
Get him!
Get him?

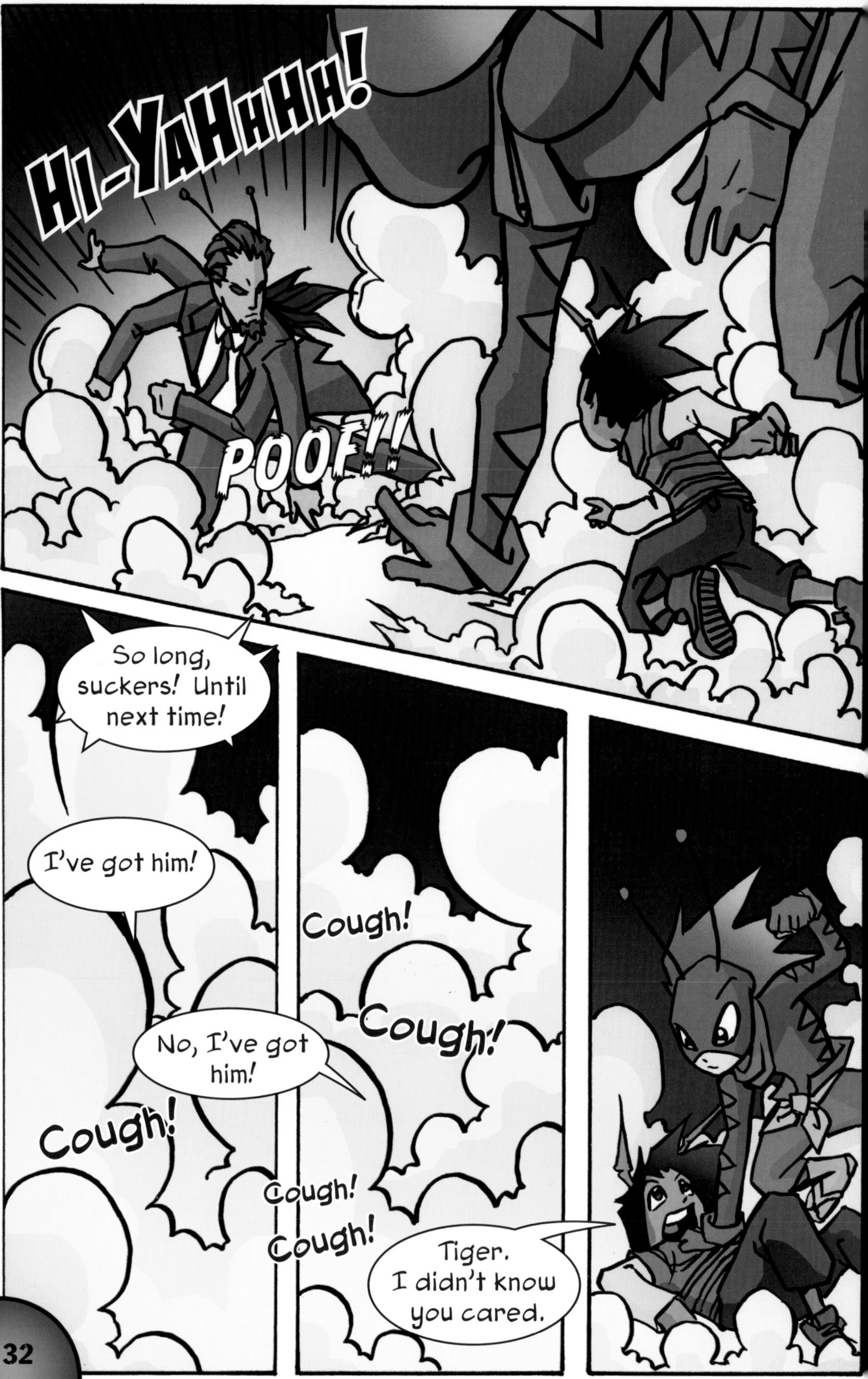
HI-YAHHHH!
POOF!!
So long, suckers! Until next time!
I've got him!
No, I've got him!
Cough!
Cough!
Cough!
Cough!
Cough!
Tiger. I didn't know you cared.

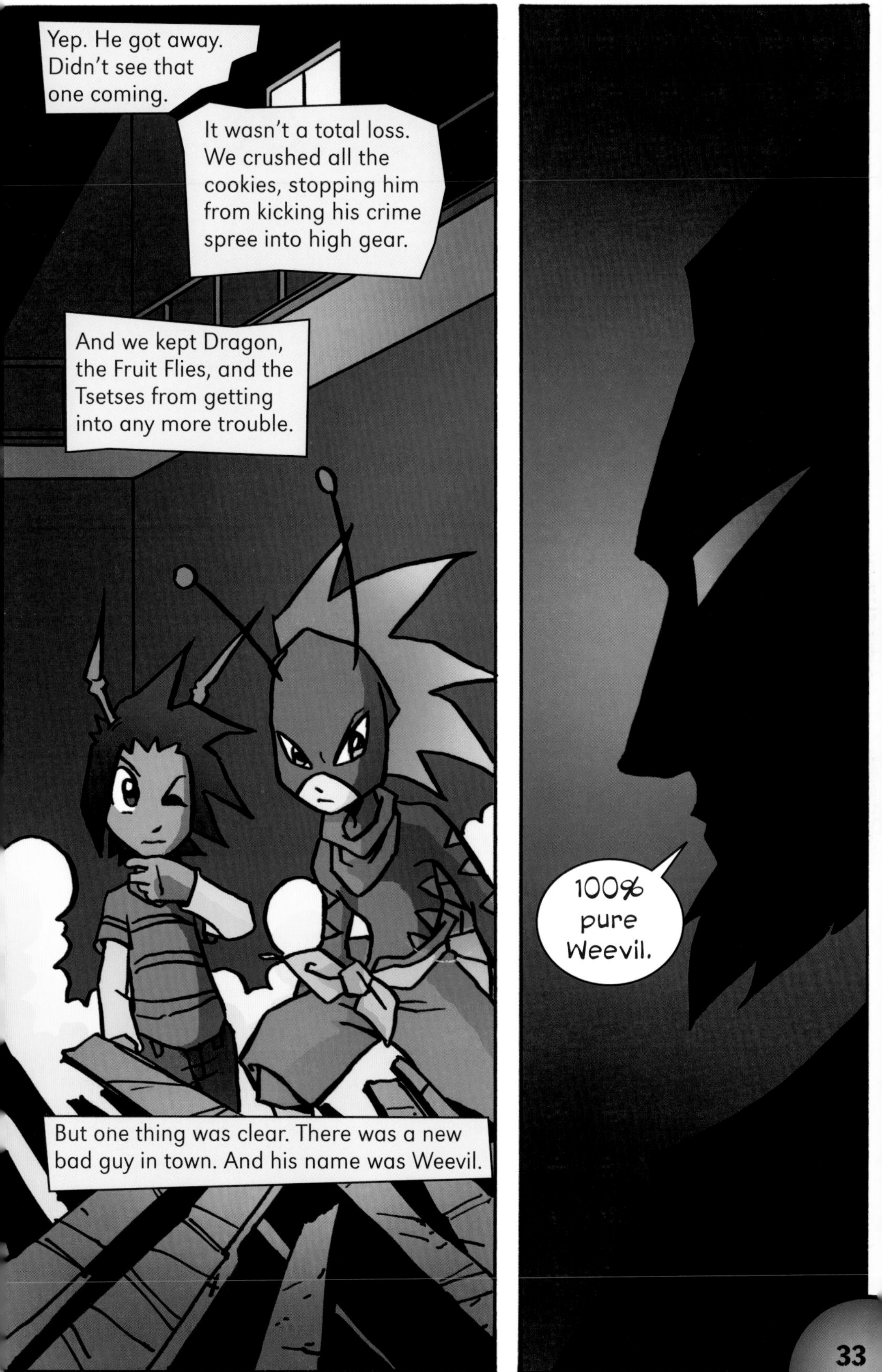
Yep. He got away. Didn't see that one coming.
It wasn't a total loss. We crushed all the cookies, stopping him from kicking his crime spree into high gear.
And we kept Dragon, the Fruit Flies, and the Tsetses from getting into any more trouble.
But one thing was clear. There was a new bad guy in town. And his name was Weevil.
100% pure Weevil.

ABOUT THE AUTHOR

Aaron Reynolds loves bugs and loves books, so Tiger Moth was a perfect blend of both. Aaron is the author of several great books for kids, including *Chicks and Salsa*, which *Publishers Weekly* called "a literary fandango" that "even confirmed macaroni-and-cheese lovers will devour." Aaron had no idea what a "fandango" was, but after looking it up in the dictionary (it means "playful and silly behavior"), he hopes to write several more fandangos in the future. He lives near Chicago with his wife, two kids, and four insect-obsessed cats.

ABOUT THE ILLUSTRATOR

Erik Lervold was born in Puerto Rico, a small island in the Caribbean, and has been a professional painter. He attended college at the University of Puerto Rico's Mayaguez campus, where he majored in Civil Engineering. Deciding that he wanted to be a full-time artist, he moved to Florida, New York, Chicago, Duluth, and finally Minneapolis. He attended the Minneapolis College of Art and Design, majored in Comic Art, and graduated in 2004. Erik teaches classes in libraries in the Minneapolis area, and has taught art in the Minnesota Children's Museum. He loves the color green and has a bunch of really big goggles. He also loves sandwiches. If you want him to be your friend, bring him a roast beef sandwich and he will love you forever.

GLOSSARY

apprentice (uh-PREN-tiss)—one who learns from someone else, just as Kung Pow learns to be a ninja from Tiger Moth

beeswax (BEEZ-waks)—a slang word for "business" as in "That's my personal beeswax!"

buffet (boo-FAY)—a big meal where people serve themselves

dojo (DOH-JOH)—a school or practice area where people and insects can learn martial arts, like karate or judo

fortune (FORT-chun)—something that might happen to you in the future

maggot (MAG-uht)—a worm, an early stage of an insect. If you find a maggot at a buffet, don't stay for dessert!

shindig (SHIN-dig)—a party

spree (SPREE)—an uncontrolled, energetic activity. Crooks go on crime sprees. Sharks go on eating sprees.

tsetse (TSEE-tsee or TEET-see)—a kind of African fly; some tsetse flies carry a form of sleeping sickness

FROM THE NINJA NOTEBOOK

Secret Messages

History is full of stories of people sending secret messages to other people. Two thousand years ago, the ancient Greeks used invisible ink to send messages between armies. They made the ink from the clear juice of plants or nuts. When the message was heated over a flame, the ink turned dark and could then be read.

During World War II, a German spy used a sweater to send a secret message. When the sweater was unraveled, the knots in the yarn stood for letters of the alphabet. The yarn could be held up against an alphabet printed on a wall, and the spy's companions could figure out the secret message.

Secret messages have also been hidden inside special containers. Hollow spaces for messages have been made inside books, shoes, pens, cameras, and even food!

During the 1970s, U.S. spies used a special container made out of the two halves of a silver dollar. The fake dollar could hold a tiny dot of film with a message printed on it. To open the coin, a spy would simply press one of the wings on the American eagle.

Sometimes spies would leave messages for each other. They would have a special place to leave them, where no one else would think of looking. The special place, or "drop point," might be a hollow brick inside a wall, a hole in a tree, or even the water tank of a restaurant's toilet. Hmmm.

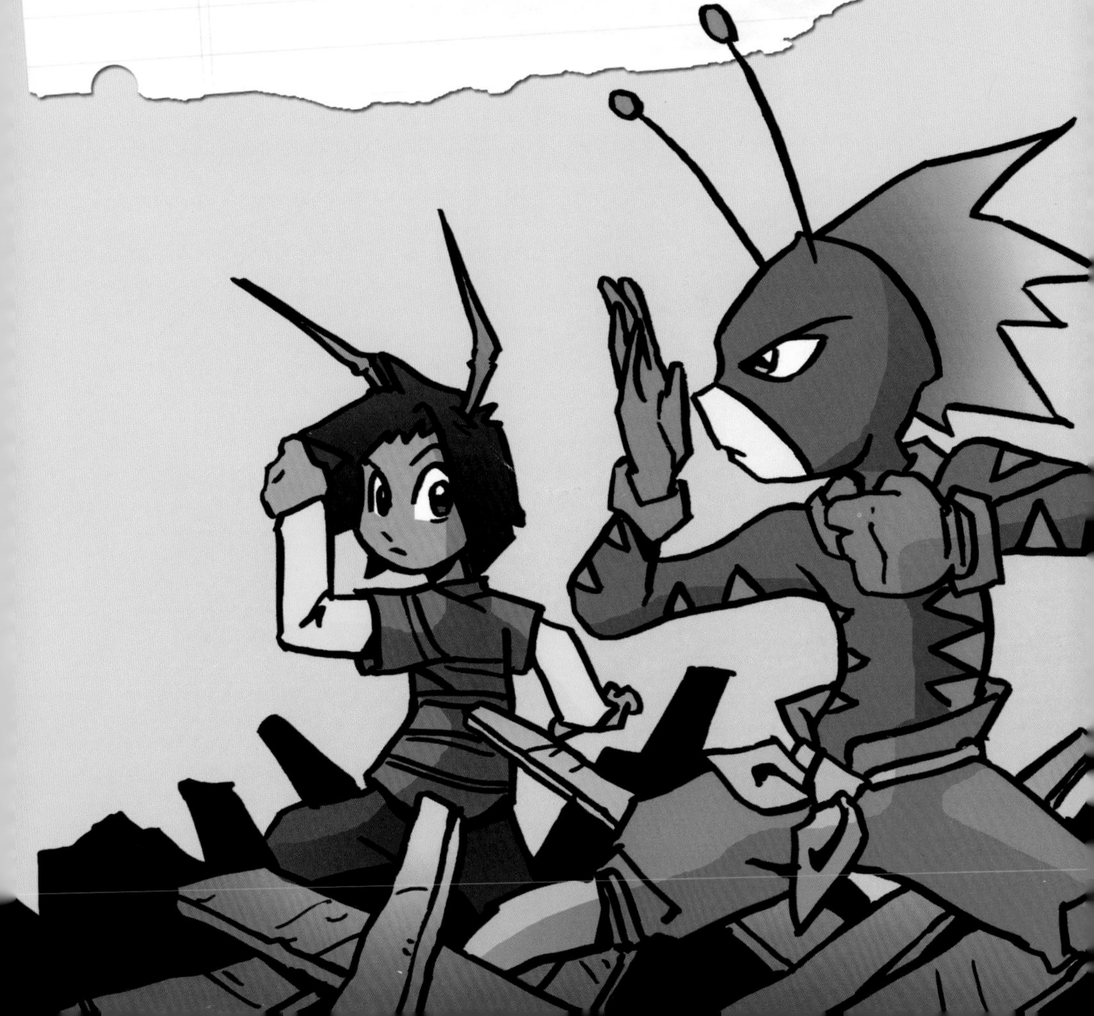

DISCUSSION QUESTIONS

1. Do you think Weevil's idea to send secret messages through fortune cookies was a good plan? Do you have a better way to send secret messages to your friends?

2. Why did Tiger Moth tell Kung Pow on page 23, "We'll work on your disguises later"?

3. Tiger Moth and Kung Pow destroy all the fortune cookies they find in Weevil's storage room. The cookies didn't belong to them. Do you think it was okay for them to destroy someone else's property? Why or why not? Would it be okay to do that in real life?

100% pure Weevil.

WRITING PROMPTS

1. Weevil escapes at the end of the story by using a smoke bomb. It looks like Weevil was prepared in case anyone tried to stop him. Tiger Moth and Kung Pow should have been better prepared, too. Write down your own ideas about how they could have stopped Weevil.

2. Do you think Weevil will come back and cause more problems for Tiger Moth? Describe what you think Weevil's next evil plan will be. Will Tiger and Kung Pow be able to stop him again?

3. Some people believe the fortunes they get from fortune cookies. Imagine that you just bought a fortune cookie from StarBugs. What does your fortune say? Write down what it is.
Does it come true?

INTERNET SITES

Do you want to know more about subjects related to this book? Or are you interested in learning about other topics? Then check out FactHound, a fun, easy way to find Internet sites.

Our investigative staff has already sniffed out great sites for you!

Here's how to use FactHound:

1. Visit www.facthound.com

2. Select your grade level.

3. To learn more about subjects related to this book, type in the book's ISBN number: 1598893181.

4. Click the **Fetch It** button.

FactHound will fetch the best Internet sites for you!